Covered

Gold Hockey #17

Elise Faber

COVERED
BY ELISE FABER
Newsletter sign-up
This is a work of fiction. Names, places, characters, and events are fictitious in every regard. Any similarities to actual events and persons, living or dead, are purely coincidental. Any trademarks, service marks, product names, or named features are assumed to be the property of their respective owners, and are used only for reference. There is no implied endorsement if any of these terms are used. Except for review purposes, the reproduction of this book in whole or part, electronically or mechanically, constitutes a copyright violation.

COVERED
Copyright © 2022 Elise Faber
Print ISBN-13: 978-1-63749-072-3
Ebook ISBN-13: 978-1-63749-071-6
Cover Art by Jena Brignola

GOLD HOCKEY SERIES

Gold Hockey (all stand alone)
Blocked
Backhand
Boarding
Benched
Breakaway
Breakout
Checked
Coasting
Centered
Charging
Caged
Crashed
A Gold Christmas
Cycled
Caught
Cap
Covered
Crushed

ONE

JORDYN

She sighed, brushing the hair off her forehead and reaching into the van for a box.

Not hers.

None of what was in front of her was hers.

It was Jess's—her future sister-in-law's—house, and her brother Josh's van. They weren't even her boxes. Not her house. Not her money because Josh had set up an account for her and the boys. Barely even her clothes, since she'd sold most of her belongings to add to her meager savings.

The boys' stuff, though, was theirs, and it would always be theirs.

She'd make certain of that.

They were going through enough, what with their father fucking their godmother, the person Jordyn had considered her best friend in the entire world. So yeah, fuck it. She would never *ever* make them give up anything, not so long as it was in her power to give it to them.

Which was why the minivan had been packed to the fucking brim with their stuff, so much so that she hadn't been able to see out the rearview on the drive down.

Her things? Gone for the most part.

A few happy memories stored away, but the rest of her belongings had been boxed away and sold so that she didn't have to think about them, didn't have to remember, didn't have to deal with what they would bring to her life.

Deal with the unhappy memories they would invoke.

All she needed was what she'd brought—a few comfortable outfits along with the couple of professional pieces she'd need to wear to find a job.

She hadn't worked in a decade, wasn't even sure what skills she might have to offer.

Not as a wife, or as a partner, in life *and* the bedroom. Daniel had made all of that abundantly clear.

She didn't know what she could offer as a woman, or hell, as an adult.

She sucked at all the roles she'd tried to step into, apparently. *All* of it.

In bed. In conversations. In—

"Everything," she whispered. "I suck at everything." A breath, or more accurately, a long, drawn-out sigh that attempted to expulse all the dark shit swirling around inside her head.

A breath to shut it out, to stop it from reappearing

A breath...that didn't make the least bit of difference in excising *any* of it.

Nope.

It was there, floating around, jabbing at her, reminding her how much of a failure she was.

Fun times.

"Beat yourself up later," she muttered, wrapping her arms around the box. Still talking to herself, yeah, but it was better than listening to that dumbass voice berating her in her own head. "Now," she whispered, "is the time to get our stuff inside the free house where the fridge is stocked with free food, kept cold because of the free utilities and"—a grunt as she hefted—"free furniture and—"

Books.

God, why did it have to be books?

Why did Marcus's prized possessions have to be books?

Probably for the same reason that Samuel's had to be Legos. Heavy, cumbersome belongings meet breakable mementos made of teeny tiny pieces that were impossible to keep together and then even more impossible to track down the evil, miniature pieces that always went missing.

And she had about eight more boxes of books to bring in.

Then at least as many of Legos.

Suitcases shoved and stacked and crammed onto the floor and passenger's seat. A cooler that had been stuffed into the limited open space in the middle row—now thankfully mostly empty of the sandwiches and drinks and snacks she'd packed for the boys. That wouldn't be heavy, at least.

Of course, it *had* fueled the frequent bathroom stops that had made the drive even longer.

Jess had been here to let them into her place, but then she'd needed to go to work.

So, Jordyn had been on her own.

Alone...

Now that was something she was used to.

Of course, she'd also promised to leave the boxes in the car because the team was coming over tomorrow and would help get her moved in.

Something she'd only agreed to because Jess had needed to go and, uh, do her freaking job.

But there was no way in hell that Jordyn was going to let Josh and his hockey team move her into the house his fiancée was letting her live in for pennies on the dollar (and not free only because Jordyn had demanded to pay at least *some* rent). The boys were asleep, their bellies full, having finally crashed after the long drive, passed out in front of the TV while watching the Gold and their uncle crush their opponents, even despite the excitement of staying at Auntie Jess's house.

So, she'd carried them into their room and tucked them into beds made up with linens she hadn't bought, walls filled with decorations that Jess and Josh had picked out for them—making it home, making it theirs, making...Jordyn bite back tears.

That was when she'd decided there was no point in sitting in a quiet, mostly empty house.

No point in sitting in the dark of the guest bedroom (because fuck all if she'd take the master from Jess, even if she was technically living with Josh now) wondering how a year ago, hell, six months ago, she'd thought her life was together and now it had all fallen apart.

A fucking mirage in the desert.

Gone like it had never been there in the first place.

"Books," she muttered, moving toward the house. "I'm focusing on books. And starting over. And it will all be fine, and the boys will be fine, and I'll be—"

The bottom tore out on the box.

Those books she was focusing on hit the ground, scattering like confetti, bouncing off her feet, and hurting like hell (*unlike* confetti). They scattered along the sidewalk, disappearing beneath the van, ricocheting into the bushes, dropping onto the damp grass.

Christ.

She dropped the box and then fell onto her knees, grabbing the books off the wet grass as fast as she could. "Fuck," she whispered, wiping Marcus's signed copy of Captain Underpants on her shirt. That was his favorite, and now the cover was wet and a little wrinkly. It'd dry, but it wouldn't ever be the same as it was before.

It would function.

It would be fine.

But it wouldn't be the same.

A breath. Another. But, *fuck*, her eyes were stinging again, and her throat had closed up, and the fucking tears, tears she hadn't let fall through the entire process of moving, of getting a lawyer, of finding her fucking best friend and husband in bed together, of trying to figure out the way forward in that aftermath, began to slip from her eyes, began to drip down her cheeks.

Then her lungs began to hitch.

Sobs rose up and instead of swallowing them down like she had managed over the past couple of months, they escaped.

And she sat there in the driveway, forehead on her knees, clutching that damned book, crying her fucking eyes out.

Until a pair of arms wrapped around her, tugging her close to a hard male body.

She fought at first.

Then figured that her brother was as stubborn as she was and had come by after his game, and anyway, her brother gave good hugs, and she was too tired to fight him, and so she slumped over, rested her head on his chest, and just...gave in.

To the strong arms.

The warm hold.

The gentle hand stroking over her hair.

But then he spoke. "You're okay."

And...

He wasn't Josh.

Scrambling, she jumped out of his hold, pushing back, lurching to her feet, staring up at the man who'd just spent the last minutes hugging her.

"What the fuck?" she gasped. "Don't touch me—"

The man was tall and big.

Much taller than her when he pushed up to standing, so much so that he practically towered over her as he found his feet. He studied her for a second, biceps pushing at the sleeves of his T-shirt, strong legs on display in his sweats.

A hockey player.

If his body hadn't given it away, the tattoos and beard would have.

And now that she got a closer look, Jordyn recognized him.

One of Josh's teammates.

B-something.

Barry? No.

Bartholomew? Nope. And her even considering that for a millisecond proved she was losing her mind.

Ben?

Better.

And also correct.

This beautiful, huge man with the shadows in his eyes, shadows that called to the ones she carried, was named Ben.

But she didn't know him, not really.

So, when he reached in, reached for her, she jerked, started to back away, but instead of touching her or taking her into his arms, he only handed her a small stack of books. Books that would have still been soaking in the grass the entire time she'd spent crying if he hadn't picked them up, she realized.

Marcus's treasures getting ruined.

Because she'd been *crying*.

Fuck.

Mutely, she took them, held them tight to her chest.

Then he turned away, and instead of leaving as she'd expected, he went to the back of the van, grabbed a box...

And walked right into the house like he owned the place.

Two

"You can't do that."

Ignoring her, he paused to wipe his feet on the mat just inside the door, continued down the hall.

"Wait. You can't just walk in here. I—Josh—you're supposed to come tomorrow."

Yeah, and by then, she would have carried all this shit in herself, and who knew how long it would take her, especially when he'd driven up and seen her crying on the driveway.

Was he supposed to be there?

No.

But...

It was one of his things, one of the techniques he used to stay calm and steady and—

Anyway, he'd given into the need, intending on just driving by so he knew where he would be going in the morning.

Then a woman collapsed in the driveway.

And sobs that wrenched through his heart.

He could no more drive on than he could stop himself from helping get those boxes inside her house. He started to set the box in the living room, intending to stack them there, figuring he'd get them in and secure so she wouldn't keep trying to do it herself.

Then tomorrow they could sort out the rest.

But when he turned toward the living room, her protests abruptly cut off.

"Those are Marcus's," she blurted. "Those are his books. I know there's a lot of them, b-but I couldn't sell them, couldn't give them away. They're his prized possessions, and I couldn't let him lose everything else and then lose—"

Her throat worked, and she turned away.

He waited.

"Those are Marcus's," she whispered again.

Shit.

That sliced through him, through his gut, his heart, his spine.

Shoring himself up, Ben made sure his voice and expression were gentle when he rotated to face her. "You want me to put it in his room?"

Because they were important to her son.

"I—" Her throat working.

He'd carry this box to the end of the world and back.

Because he had a mother who would do anything for her son, for *him*.

And because he was standing in front of a woman who would do anything for *her* son.

It would be *nothing* for him to bring the boxes into that bedroom.

"N-no, of course not. Putting it there is fine."

"You sure?"

She shook her head, her next words coming out in a flurry of sputter. "Y-you—no, that's okay. He's—they're both in there. I mean, they sleep like the dead—they both do. I swear"—she laughed and it prickled down his spine—"they would sleep through a hurricane."

He started to bend.

"And anyway," she went on, words still coming out in a rush.

"You must be tired. The boys watched the game—I did, too. It was a good one, but tough and—and it's late, and you just had to deal with a sobbing, crazy woman on the driveway, so you should just leave the box there and go home to rest and—"

She broke off, jaw clenching together, as though to stop the flow of words.

Right.

It would be easy enough for him to carry the box to the room.

He turned, moved down the hall, leaving her to gather herself as he poked his head in the doors—an office with a desk and armchair and a wall of mostly-empty shelves; a larger bedroom with a king-sized bed and en suite which was empty; a guest room with several duffle bags on the bed, as though she would be staying there instead of the bigger bedroom.

Weird.

But he was still moving, and the next room proved to be almost as big as the larger bedroom, and there were two beds, two sleeping boys inside, their forms clearly illuminated by a book-shaped nightlight.

His heart squeezed at the sight of the blankets tucked up over them, pajama-clad arms and legs hanging out from beneath the material.

Sleeping. Like the dead.

Which meant they didn't move as he slipped through the door and carefully set the box of books by the bookshelves.

Then he turned and went back out into the hall, nearly mowing Jordyn over, not having heard her come up behind him. He caught her arms when she tried to lurch out of his way, steadying her.

And just as quickly releasing her.

Because he knew about the soon-to-be ex-husband.

Because he knew she was vulnerable and alone and hurt.

Because he knew what it was like to go through the same.

The rest of the boxes didn't take long at all—they were labeled —and he brought the heavy crates of books, the unbalanced containers of Legos into the boys' bedroom, stacking them on their respective sides.

Easy to see considering the bedspreads.

The Lego Movie emblazoned on the younger one's—for Samuel. A book character on Marcus's.

They didn't have much, just a few boxes each, the duffles he'd seen in the guest room. A cooler she'd brought in, a few containers in the kitchen, in the living room.

But most of the house had Jess's touch.

Because Jordyn had been left with nothing.

A wave of protectiveness coiled inside him. He'd grown up with a deadbeat dad who'd disappeared when he was eight, emptying bank accounts, leaving his mom as a single mom to him and his sister.

He *knew* how hard it was to scrape out an existence.

Because *he'd* had to scrape that existence out.

Because his mom hadn't been like Jordyn. She hadn't fought for them. She'd—

He shook his head, not wanting to revisit old nightmares.

They were dark enough that when Josh had asked if anyone was free to help out with the move, Ben had quickly volunteered. He would have helped anyway, because the team was family, but having heard what was going down, there was no way Ben wouldn't have been *right* here.

Though, he'd been planning on being *right here* in the morning.

Didn't matter.

He was glad he'd come.

He reached into the van, snagged the last box—labeled pictures—and carried it into the house.

Those he deposited in the living room.

He retraced his steps, stopping in the doorway of the kitchen, seeing that Jordyn was rinsing out a cooler.

"The van's empty."

Her spine stiffened, and slowly, she reached for the faucet, turning it off.

When she rotated to face him, the look on her face hit him with the force of a Mack truck.

Pain.

Memories.

His past.

His mother.

"Thanks," she said softly, wiping her hands on a towel.

Then she bit her lip, and he found himself moving toward her, telling himself that he would stop if she showed the slightest bit of hesitation at his closeness, if she retreated.

But she stayed in place, watched him approach.

So carefully, so carefully, he reached up and ran the back of his knuckles across her cheek. "No thanks needed, sweetpea."

She was sweet.

God, she was sweet. And sad.

What would it take to make her smile?

He was going to find out. He knew that much.

"You should go," she whispered. "It's late, and you must be tired."

He wasn't tired, hadn't been from the moment he'd wrapped her in his arms, the moment that was now seared in his brain.

She'd felt...right.

She'd felt like *his*.

But he didn't have any other reason to stay, and it *was* late, and she had shadows under her eyes.

She needed him to go.

She needed to rest.

She needed—he hoped—to not cry herself to sleep, like his mom had done so many nights, smothering the noise with a pillow.

But he'd heard anyway.

Which was probably why he touched her cheek again, felt that silken skin beneath his fingers. Probably why he started to ask the next question, "Do you—"

He clamped his teeth together.

She didn't *know* him. He didn't have the right to ask her about—

"What?" she whispered, not backing away, not retreating from his touch. "What were you going to ask?"

Ben might have ignored the question, made his excuses, and left, if not for the curiosity in her eyes.

So, he gave it to her.

Something he had the feeling he was going to be doing a lot of, and not just because of what his mother had gone through, not because he had empathy for Jordyn's situation.

Not even because of her beauty—and she was *gorgeous*. Light brown skin, chocolate-colored eyes, hair he was desperate to sink his hands into, a body that was curvy and delicious.

But none of that was what was already pulling him in. None of that explained the inexorable draw that he knew wouldn't be easy to escape, one that he probably wouldn't *want* to escape.

Because...*right.*

Holding her had felt right.

Helping her felt right.

Standing here, talking to her, no matter how stilted, felt right.

So, he stepped a little closer, cupped her jaw, thumb brushing over that soft skin again, and he asked the question that he didn't have the right to ask, asked the question he had no logical reason to *want* to know the answer to, "Do you think you'll be able to sleep tonight, sweetpea?"

THREE

"Do you think you'll be able to sleep tonight, sweetpea?"

Her lungs expanded on the endearment, just a big breath in, held.

Long enough for her lungs to burn, for her to realize that she hadn't actually let the air out, and that she needed to because otherwise the spots that had begun to appear at the edges of her vision would expand, would black everything out, and—

She didn't want to miss a minute of this man.

Which was a thought that had all the breath bursting out of her lungs in a rapid exhale.

Because...where the fuck had it come from?

It had been six months.

Six months since she'd gone from happy and content to sad and alone and—

Single.

She wavered on her feet, suddenly exhausted and scared and sad and alone and—

Realizing in that one moment—the barest hint of interest in

someone who wasn't Daniel, that there was nothing stopping her from pursuing that interest.

That she was free.

Fuck. Why was there a blip of relief there? Of happy?

She was sick.

She was *happy* her marriage had imploded? That her boys' father was a douchebag who'd made it clear he had limited interest in being in their lives.

Want to move away? Sure. I'll sign off on that.

That was what he'd said.

Sure. I'll sign off on that.

And on the first day here in California...relief.

Her knees shook.

Threatened to give way.

Ben caught her arms, drew her toward him, and she hardly knew this man, but she still let him draw her against his chest, to hug her tightly.

Stupid. But he was Josh's friend.

And he looked at her like he actually saw her.

And...she hadn't had that in a long time.

And...maybe she hadn't *ever* had it.

So, for a moment, she gave in to the urge to let Ben hold her, allowed herself to sink into his warmth, his strength, the spicy scent of him in her nose, and with that bit of giving in, she found herself saying, "No," she whispered. "I don't really sleep. Not anymore."

He went stiff, arms tightening. "Jordyn," he whispered, and there was something heavy in it.

As though the truth hurt him, when it made no sense for it to bother him in the least.

Maybe...maybe he was just really empathetic.

Maybe that was what she could use to make sense of this moment, of this man.

But there was a niggle in her mind, one that was telling her this wouldn't be all that simple.

She ignored it for the moment, called up her strength, the strength that had carried her through her separation, breaking the news to the boys, facing the knowing look of the parents at school when she went to pick them up, selling all her things, packing up, making the drive.

She was exhausted, worn down to the bone.

They'd gotten through the move. Now she just needed to unpack and finish setting up the house and, of course, get her boys registered for school, find new doctors for all of them, set up sports and extracurriculars, organize playdates so they had new friends here, since they'd left their old friends behind and...

School supplies.

Sports uniforms.

New shoes and pants for Marcus since he'd outgrown his current ones.

Planning a party for Sam, since his birthday was coming up, and it was the first celebration they were having without their dad, not at home, without those old friends, which meant that she was going to have to make it *extra* special.

Which meant that she needed to do invites and decorations and food and cake and candles and presents and party favors.

But, more importantly, she needed to be able to pay for all of that.

So, she had to get a job.

Which also meant that she had to sort out childcare.

Another expense.

Another thing to figure out.

Another fucking responsibility.

And all of those responsibilities together were heavy, were so fucking heavy that it was like they had all dropped onto her shoulders and made it feel like she had suddenly been left carrying a giant ass boulder. It was a lot and too much and overwhelming, but she shoved the weight of all that she had to do away.

Shoved it down.

One step at a time.

That was how she had been getting through everything—just one step at a time, focusing on the small things.

That was what let her straighten then, to pull out of that warm, strong hold, to stand on her own feet and not waver.

Her chin came up. "I'll be okay."

"I know." No hesitation.

Not one second of it.

Her lips parted, brows tugging together. "You seem sure," she murmured the next moment.

He brushed his knuckles over her cheek again, and hell if that touch didn't make her feel like those boulders had grown a little lighter. His words, though, they made it seem like the boulder had disappeared entirely. "I see you," he said, brushing over her skin again. "I see you."

She exhaled and it was shaky.

But her legs remained steady, and her knees didn't shake and—

A warm palm cupping her jaw. "Since you're not going to sleep, do you want to watch some TV?"

Since that was pretty much the last thing she'd expected to come out of his mouth—hell, this whole night had been unexpected, her last weeks, last months had been unexpected.

She sat in that unexpected, sat in the surprise his words brought.

So that was probably why she didn't protest when he took her hand and led her to the living room.

Let him draw her from the kitchen, let him nudge her down onto the couch.

He handed her the remote and disappeared out the front door, and for a second, that *unexpected* cleared and she figured she'd heard wrong, that he'd been encouraging her to watch TV until she got tired and fell asleep, not that they'd watch together.

Clearly, she'd been reaching.

Thinking that he would stay.

Stupid.

She hit the button for the remote, turned on the TV, just as she heard the front door open again.

Probably coming to tell her to lock up.

But instead, he moved to the kitchen, and she heard the water running. He was...finishing up with the cooler, she realized when the sound of it being moved around the inside of the sink, jostled against the edges, that hollow plastic noise as it was bumped reaching her ears.

She hadn't gotten any further than just turning on the TV when he walked back into the living room.

"Scoot," he said, sitting right next to her on the small couch, shifting her to the side, and taking up altogether too much room.

Even with her *scooting,* their legs were still touching.

That was more...unexpected.

Especially with how his thigh pressed to hers, how warm he was, how strong and spicy and *male* he was.

Then he was leaning close, and her heart was thudding, but even as she was processing both of those, he snagged the remote from her hand.

Her lungs seized.

"What do you like to watch?"

All she could do was shrug.

His mouth tipped up. "You know"—those knuckles touched her cheek again—"the guys always tease me for being quiet, but you have me beat, don't you?"

She wasn't quiet.

Or she hadn't been, not normally.

Not growing up.

Not until she'd gotten married.

Then...she'd gotten even more and more quiet.

She inhaled.

She wasn't going to think of that, not right now.

A chuckle. "You definitely have me beat."

"I wasn't," she whispered, glancing up at him. The bristles on his jaw, the hazel eyes, his deep brown hair. "I didn't used to be quiet."

His nostrils flared on an inhale. "What changed?"

"My marriage."

Gentle on his face, sparks in his eyes. "He ever get physical with you?"

"No." A shake of her head. "He didn't hit me or hurt me *that* way"—an emphasis on *that* because he'd hurt her in other ways, plenty of other ways—"he just...disappeared."

He stilled.

"Not at first. God, he was a great dad at first. But then he got a different job and started traveling for work." She sighed. "I quit my position because he was making so much more, and I needed to be home with the boys. And then—I can't really pinpoint it— at some point, he began pulling back."

And at some point, she'd gotten quiet.

And...now she didn't need to be.

Those knuckles on her cheek again. His next question dragging her out of her memories. "What do you like to watch?"

She blinked, shrugging off the near mental whiplash. "What?"

A nod toward the TV.

Oh.

What did she want to watch?

Fuck, if she had any idea.

She didn't have time to watch TV—and if she did, it was either the boys putting on some crappy cartoon or YouTube video, or the three of them watching the Gold.

Ben's lips twitched, seeming to hear that thought.

"How about..."

He named some movie she'd never seen.

"Okay."

A couple of presses on the remote and it was streaming through the TV, and—no offense to the man—it was absolutely boring.

Horrible.

Dragging.

So freaking slow that she found herself slumping back on the couch.

So freaking slow that her lids slipped closed.

Then she fell asleep.

Four

In fairness to the woman who'd just slumped against him, fully asleep, she'd lasted way longer than he'd expected.

The movie was trash.

He'd seen it with his little sister and mom the last time they'd gotten together, before everything had gotten really bad with his sister before—

He shook himself, ignoring the pain that came from thinking about Maddy, about how her life had gone so completely off the rails. Instead, he'd thought about paying $12.50 per fucking ticket for that awful fucking moving, and more than that for snacks.

But his sister had wanted to see it.

So, he'd taken them and he hadn't even passed out during the showing.

Go him.

But the trashy movie and its supremely boring qualities were something he'd banked on tonight. It was well after midnight, closing in on two thirty in the morning, actually.

If her boys were anything like he'd been at that age, they would be up and raring to go the moment the sun began to rise.

Which meant that Jordyn would be in for a rude awakening in a few hours.

The protective core of him needed to make sure she got as much sleep as possible.

So, movie.

Check.

Droopy eyelids.

Check.

Fully asleep.

Finally...*check.*

Now he just needed to stay awake long enough to make sure she was fully asleep before he slipped out.

Which was going to be a nightmare with this fucking movie.

So, he carefully grabbed the remote, switched to something more interesting—at least for him.

Fishing.

And when the guys on screen had caught the *big one*, and Jordyn was still slumped against him, her breathing steady, her body heavy as it pressed to his, her lids closed, the thick lashes on her eyes resting against her cheeks, he decided that he'd waited long enough.

Carefully, he shifted off the couch, bent to scoop her up, and carried her down to the guest bedroom.

It wasn't easy to hold her while using one hand to turn on the lights, to flip back the covers, to drag the duffles off the mattress and drop them on the floor.

But then the bags were out of the way and there was a space to lie her down.

So he did, tucking the blankets back over her.

He took a moment to snag the duffles, to stash them in a corner on the far side of the bed so they wouldn't be a tripping hazard.

Then he turned off the lights, closed the door halfway.

TV off, living room lights off, the back door locked.

Finding a spare set of keys by digging through the kitchen drawers, he walked outside, locked up, and checked the van.

Since that was open, he pressed the button inside to lock *those* doors.

Only then was he satisfied that she and the boys inside the house would be safe.

Only then did he move to his car and get inside.

Only then did he drive home, walk into his empty house, and get ready for bed.

But he didn't sleep.

Not for a long, long time.

———

His alarm came way too fucking early.

But he knew that Josh and the rest of the guys would be heading to Jordyn's place, and he needed to be there to help.

Needed to be there to see her.

Needed—

To stop thinking so hard, get his ass in the shower, and get moving.

He inhaled, scrubbed his hands over his face.

Then released it slowly.

Then he got his ass into the shower, got dressed, and got moving.

En route to Jordyn's place, he made a pit stop at a donut place—grabbing a couple dozen, knowing that even if one of the guys brought some, kids loved donuts and hockey players did too, especially since today was a Cheat Day.

One of the things that made the Gold so successful was their support staff.

They had excellent trainers, great coaching—which included everything from off-ice conditioning to skating to video review to actual on-ice coaching and strategy. Management had also recently taken the Breakers' lead and hired a sports psychologist, and she'd made it clear that she would be available to speak with them whenever they needed. The players also had team doctors who were on call twenty-four seven for anything physical that popped up. Plus, on practice and game days, they had tasty and healthy food available that fit the individual meal plans the team's nutritionist had created for each of them. And there was probably more than that, but it was the butt crack of dawn and he'd had like three hours of sleep, so that was all he could think of at the moment.

Basically anything he and the other players could possibly think of, they had been given.

And they were consistently a competitor; consistency produced.

Had fans who were rabidly loyal, a great outreach arm with the community, and, well, it was a fucking great place to play.

Ben had never expected to get here at all.

But to get to play with the *Gold*, to be a part of *this* organization?

He felt like Cinderella on that cold night, his fairy godmother having appeared to work some magic.

And it could disappear in an instant.

The stakes were high for a player like him.

He was old for a rookie, having played college first and completing his business degree. Then he'd made his way up through the professional ranks, ECHL to AHL and finally to the Gold. But he hadn't been a top pick for the team. The only reason he'd been invited to rookie training camp at all—a clinic the team put on so the younger guys could get a feel for playing in the league—when he was old enough to be the other prospects' grandpa (which was an exaggeration, but he *was* an ancient twenty-seven) was because one of the other guys had been injured and he happened to be visiting family who lived in the Bay Area.

But he'd brought his best effort, like he did every single time he played, and he'd turned that one opportunity into a roster spot.

It wasn't new for him.

Ben hadn't been scouted for college, hadn't gotten a scholarship or offers to play in the juniors.

Playing in the NHL had always seemed to be just a few inches out of reach.

But his drive had been there. He'd made his college team as a walk-on. He'd fought through to play with the Gold now.

It was good now.

Great even.

He was just...critically aware of how easy it would be for it all to be taken away.

So, that was always in the back of his head.

Even with a three-year contract in place and big-league money in his account, there was a part of him that was always on guard, always prepared for it to be taken away.

The opportunity.

The team.

The family they'd built.

He knew it wasn't reasonable. He knew he'd earned his spot.

But he couldn't stop the thoughts from reappearing time and again in his mind.

Because...his own security, his own family had been torn from him, from his mother, from his sister.

So, he understood just how easily the sands of fate could shift.

Could blow away.

Could disappear.

"Will that be all?"

He blinked, glancing up at the woman working behind the counter at the donut shop. She was taping the box of two dozen donuts closed, waiting for him to answer the question.

His gaze hit the fridge behind her.

And he realized what he was missing.

"Oh, no," he said, mentally tallying the number of kids that would probably descend on Jordyn's house—it would be a gaggle, no doubt. "Can you add six of the chocolate milks?" A beat. "Oh, and four regular," he added, realizing that while chocolate milk had been one of his favorite treats when he was the boys' age, there might be some non-chocolate kids in that gaggle.

Blasphemy.

But...kids these days.

Grinning, he paid for the donuts and milk, headed back out to his car, and by the time he made it to Jordyn's, a few cars were parked on the street and in the driveway.

He parked, got out, and was just making it up the walkway as he heard Josh grumble, "I told you to wait for me, Jorie."

"I was fine." Her gaze slid beyond her brother's and connected with his, as though asking if he wanted to keep last night to himself.

No one should be stupid enough to hide anything about Jordyn.

She was beautiful and smart and kind and—

Her brows lifted.

He shrugged.

Lips twitching, she glanced back at her brother. "I was fine," she said. "And it wasn't all that many boxes," she went on, leaving Ben's involvement out. Probably for the best. He didn't think Josh would be all that thrilled with the idea of a teammate hanging out into the wee hours of the morning with his sister. "Plus"—she nudged her brother's shoulder with her own—"you know the worst part is actually unpacking the boxes."

"Stubborn." Josh sighed and then wrapped an arm around her, turning her and guiding her back into the house.

"Stubborn is as stubborn does."

Another sigh, but Josh let his sister slip out of his hold and disappear down the hall. Then glanced back at Ben. "Hey."

A nod. "Hey."

Josh's gaze went to the box in Ben's hand, to the bag he held, and Ben didn't miss the curiosity blooming to life in Josh's brown eyes.

Curiosity *and* wariness.

As though he could see exactly what Ben thought of his sister, could see right through the calm aura he was trying to project.

As though he knew *exactly* what Ben had dreamed of last night.

Silken skin. Curves that called for his hands, his mouth. Lips that he needed to kiss.

Josh cleared his throat.

Shit.

Those eyes narrowed.

He braced.

"Uncle Josh!" came two loud voices, two pairs of feet pounding on the floor.

Then Jordyn's boys were wrapping their arms around their uncle's waist, at least until one of them glanced over at Ben and noticed the box he was carrying.

"Donuts!" he yelled, distracting his uncle.

Ben released a breath.

Saved by pastries.

He'd take it.

FIVE

"Your uncle is here," she'd told her sleepy boys, their little bodies still in their pajamas, their hair mussed and faces crinkled from the hard sleep of the night before.

They'd been awake for a little bit, but moving slowly, and she knew the feeling.

Her eyes were crusty. Her shoulders and arms sore as hell.

Not just from the boxes, but from the drive itself, from clutching the steering wheel tightly as she weaved through the mountain roads that led down from Oregon to California, keeping them in their lane through the windy stretches of highway that had threatened to push their van off the road.

But Josh was here and so was Stefan and Brit, the Gold's former captain and the Gold's current goalie, respectively, Blane and Mandy, a retired defenseman and the current head trainer, Coop and Calle, Gold forward and offensive coach, Blue and Anna, another forward and his wife who wasn't related to the organization in any way aside from her relationship with Blue. A few of the others were supposed to come, but not until later—a combination of kids actually sleeping in for once, of having to get up early for sports activities, and of not having kids, so able to sleep in.

Ah, peaceful oblivion.

Hopefully that was what Jess was experiencing.

She was mom to a newborn and working hard, and Jordyn knew a bit about that.

So, when Josh had pressed a kiss to her cheek that morning, murmured, "Jess will be by later," she'd understood.

Of course she had, would have, even if they hadn't already done so much for her.

They'd been her sounding board, her support system, her financial aid, and rescuers.

She hated that she and her boys were so vulnerable, that Daniel was fighting her every step of the way in providing for his children—even while flaunting his relationship on social media, complete with fancy vacations and restaurant selfies and a new sports car.

Yup.

She wasn't even thirty yet, and her ex-husband was having a midlife crisis...a third life crisis? A quarter life crisis?

Third.

Third.

Because she highly doubted he was going to live to one hundred and twenty.

If the fates were kind—

No, she wouldn't even think that, wouldn't wish that on her boys.

She hoped that Daniel would get his shit together—not back with her, that ship had long since sailed, but maybe he'd understand the gift he was missing out on by not being there for Marcus and Sam.

Hope.

Maybe it was stupid.

Maybe she should be excising that hope from her heart, not allowing it to come back in.

But...she'd lived her life growing quieter and quieter.

It was time to stop that, time to stop cramming her emotions into increasingly smaller boxes, time to let go, move on, and live her life, making sure her boys did the same.

But she would never *ever* believe in shutting down that hope.

Her boys needed it, and so did she.

She rubbed Marcus's back. "You want to go say hello?"

He nodded, though his face was still in his pillow, and what she did next spoke to the hope still firmly entrenched in her heart.

She shifted positions, moved to Samuel's bed, and told her baby, "You want to see Uncle Josh?"

Never did she make things competitive with the boys.

That only made her the referee, and she didn't always succeed in implementing Webb house rules (number one of which was, namely, that disputes were handled by playing a round of UNO whenever possible...and for her boys, that meant dispute handling via UNO happened often enough for her to despise the game).

But she'd seen the way Ben was looking at her as he'd walked up to the house.

She knew Josh would see it too.

And...what had happened last night—the boxes, the kitchen, the couches, waking up in her bed, tucked beneath the cover—felt like a delicate flower just beginning to open.

Fragile.

Beautiful.

Vulnerable.

Especially to protective older brothers.

"Uncle Josh is here?" Sammy asked, rubbing at his eyes.

"Yup," she said gently. "And he needs hugs, big man."

Alertness in his gaze. "I'm good at hugs."

And here she inserted a dash of competitiveness. "The *best* hugs."

"The *best* hugs," he agreed.

"Nu-uh," Marcus said, sitting up. "*I* give the best hugs."

"Hurry," she intervened. "He needs hugs from both of you. He's feeling lonely because Auntie Jessie isn't here."

The competition then included dashing out of bed and down the hall and yelling her brother's name.

Luckily, he was here to play UNO with them if the match turned feral.

Luckily, they were still young enough for distraction to work.

Luckily, she'd seen a big box of donuts in Ben's hands.

————

She reached into a cabinet, pulled out a stack of plates (Jess's since Jordyn's had been sold), and brought them over to the kids along with the box of donuts.

"Just one," she murmured to her boys.

They were good boys.

But they gave her puppy dog eyes when she put that limit in place.

"If there are extras, you can have another." She ruffled Marcus's hair. "You know we need to let everyone"—she glanced at the other kids behind them who'd come with their parents, a mix of sleepy and awake and some still in their jammies like her boys were (though they were all positively vibrating with excitement at the prospect of donuts)—"have a chance first before we do seconds."

Marcus made a face, but he nodded and chose one of the sprinkle donuts.

No surprise there.

Hell, she was a grown woman and *still* wanted the one with sprinkles.

Samuel went with sprinkles too.

Then they brought their pajama-clad bodies over to the

couch, slumping down in them and pounding those donuts like the champs they were. Cartoons were on in the background, the rest of the kids gathered around with their donuts, and it was a sweet morning scene.

Her heart squeezed.

Her boys could have this.

Could be *part* of this family the Gold had built.

Or maybe, she thought as Anna brought the milk cartons into the room and began doling them out, they already were.

Through Josh.

Through Jess.

Through—

"You should grab one, too."

Ben.

She blinked, turned to the man who was standing close to her shoulder, sending a tendril of heat down her spine. "What?"

He nodded at the box, at the big ole hockey players who were descending on the treats like the Cheat Day it was. "You might not get your first choice."

A shrug. "I'll survive."

He frowned.

"It's all fried dough topped with frosting." She smiled up at him. "I'm not going to complain, no matter what I get."

That frown deepened. "Which is your favorite?"

That flower in her chest unfurled a little more.

"Maple bar."

A nod, started to turn toward the box. "Mapl—" He paused and looked back at her. "Maple bar, *really?*"

"You got a problem with that?" she asked, and hell if she didn't surprise herself with the bit of the tart that entered her tone. Daniel hadn't liked it when she sassed him, so eventually she'd stopped doing it. Eventually she'd been too tired and worn down to *keep* doing it. "I like what I like."

A glance that sent a shiver through her.

"Plus, the benefit to liking something disgusting that no one else likes is that there's always at least one left," Josh chimed in.

"Hey," she sputtered.

Josh winked. "I only speak the truth, Jorie."

God, she hated that nickname.

The only reason she didn't protest it any longer was because of how Josh's voice sounded when he called her that.

She still narrowed her eyes at him.

Grinning, he picked up a plate and handed it to Ben.

Who cut the line of adults now queueing patiently for their turn at the donuts, reached into the box, and grabbed out a maple bar.

Stupidly, her heart was pounding. Thudding against her ribs as he walked back toward her, thumping against them as she inhaled and caught a whiff of his scent.

"Here," he murmured.

"Thanks," she whispered back, because that was the only volume she could manage.

The plate hit her hands. Her heart was still pounding.

His knuckles brushed her cheek.

She inhaled sharply.

"Eat, sweetpea."

It was a gentle order, and maybe she should have rebuked it, should have put a hard stop to him giving her any orders right then and there.

But...

It was gentle, and his eyes were warm, and he'd touched her cheek so softly—

She took a bite of donut.

And another.

And another.

And it was only when she'd finished the donut that she realized it was the first time in months that she'd done that.

That she'd cleared her plate.

Finished a meal, as incomplete one donut was as a meal.

It was the first time she'd eaten in months and hadn't felt sick to her stomach.

It was...the first time she'd felt like herself.

No, she thought.

It was the *second* time.

Because the first had been with Ben last night on the couch, sitting and watching that godawful movie.

Six

Ben

He avoided Josh's gaze, understanding that his eyes would probably reveal too much, as he snagged a plate and moved to the back of the line.

By the time he made it up to the box, *his* favorite was gone.

Chocolate cake donut with chocolate glaze (and chocolate sprinkles, because why the fuck not? Sprinkles were the shit).

He made do with a chocolate glazed then made a pit stop by the coffee pot.

Jordyn filled a mug for him. "How do you take it?"

"A spoon of sugar and a dash of cream."

A nod and she added the ingredients then refilled her cup.

"Black?" he asked, brows raised.

"Puts hair on my chest," she quipped.

Josh leaned on the counter next to her, lifted his mug, eyes pleading, and with a heavy, sisterly sigh that Ben himself had heard often over the years, Jordyn set her cup down, snagged his, and filled it for him, adding cream and sugar with a heavy hand.

Then she passed it over. "You're lucky I love you."

He tugged her hair. "You're lucky I love *you*."

Soft on her face, rising on tiptoe to press a kiss to her brother's cheek. "Yeah," she whispered. "I am."

Josh wrapped an arm around her, hugged her tight. "I'm the lucky one."

"Sap," she teased.

"Damn right."

Jordyn dropped back down onto her heels, and returned to her own coffee, sucking it back in a way that Ben highly identified with.

Sweet, sweet sustenance.

"Okay," she said after she'd finished her mug and set it on the counter. "Where do we start?"

Brit came over, joining their little circle. "Kitchen," she said. "Always the kitchen."

"You're just saying that because there isn't much to unpack," Josh said.

Brit rolled her shoulder. "Gotta keep this baby ready to catch all the pucks."

Josh snorted, though Ben knew it was probably more from Brit's antics than the inaccuracy of that statement. Brit's stats were impressive, even knowing this was her final year in the league (or at least, that was what she was telling everyone right now—who knew what would happen when it came time to actually *officially* retire?). Regardless of whether or not that retirement actually happened, Ben knew that Brit was still a contender in the league, stiff shoulder or not.

Her goals against average had been in the top five for the last decade, and her save percentage was high enough that she was a regular at the All-Star Game.

Not flashy or showy.

No drama.

No big peaks and valleys, just good, consistent playing and hard-ass work, fighting her way up through the ranks and then taking advantage of any opportunities that came her way.

And luck.

Luck always played a role in this journey.

Something Ben could identify with.

"Better not miss any glove side," Josh muttered. Then he sighed, put his mug into the sink, and started giving out orders like the captain he was. "Stefan and Brit, Blane and Mandy," he called, "you're on the boys' room." A sly look toward their goaltender. "You can rest that shoulder by sorting Legos."

"Sweet Christ," Brit muttered, but she didn't argue further, just headed out of the kitchen.

"Anna, Blue, and I will be on living room duty."

Anna saluted and disappeared.

A nod to Ben. "You're on kitchen duty. And you"—he glanced at his sister, lips twitching—"you're going to move your stuff into the master." A beat. "Either *that*," he added as Ben watched the protest well up on Jordyn's face, "or I'll call Jess, wake her up, and get her to kick your ass down the hall. It makes no sense for the boys to share when there are three bedrooms."

Since Ben had wondered about that, he didn't move, other than to pretend to straighten up the donut mess (and steal another chocolate glazed).

"They *want* to share," Jordyn said, her voice shaking just the slightest bit. "They need each other with everything that—"

"So use the guest bedroom as a guest bedroom."

She snorted. "Who's going to visit? If Mom and Dad come, they would stay with you. Jeremy definitely would. My friends—"

That wobble increased.

Christ.

Ben couldn't handle that.

He moved a little closer, pretending to wash mugs, but really, he was taking the opportunity to gently brush his arm against hers.

She didn't back away.

So, he stayed there, arm close to hers.

Jordyn blew out a breath.

And Josh must have sensed how close she was to breaking

because his voice gentled. "So keep it as an office. Look for something you can work from home at. The boys will be in school during the day, so there won't be any interruptions and then you wouldn't have to worry about childcare."

Jordyn shifted and Ben glanced over his shoulder to see that her head had come up.

He watched her body relax.

"That's a good idea," she whispered. "That's a really, really good idea."

"Glad you think so," he said. "And we're hiring a nanny—I'll make sure she's open to the occasional babysitting of my nephews. I want our kiddos to be close, and I want you to have backup and the opportunity for a break."

"And you have all of us," Ben chimed in.

It wasn't his place to talk.

But he'd finished with the mugs and couldn't continue pretending to clean out the sink.

For one, it was spotless.

For another, the entire state was in a drought and that was wasteful.

Whatever you want to tell yourself, baby.

Always his mother's voice. Anytime his brain wanted to call him on his bullshit, it was always in his mother's voice.

Probably because that was the only way it got through.

Josh glanced up and there was approval in his eyes—though that approval would probably be decidedly less apparent if he knew what Ben was thinking about when it came to Josh's sister.

He didn't have time to focus on that because Jordyn was rotating to face him, questions on her face.

"We all chip in," he said. "We all watch each other's backs and step in when we see one of us struggling. You can do your own thing," he told her when concern joined the questions. "We're a nosy, pushy bunch, but we won't step into your space unless you need it." A breath. "But we're here. You're Josh's, and so you're ours. The boys, too. Anything you need—babysitting, cleaning the gutters, taking the boys to practice. *Anything.*"

He was framing it like that offer was coming from the entire team.

But he was making that offer from *him*, from his heart and soul.

Jordyn's chin dropped, gaze falling away from him, but he hadn't missed the glimmer in her eyes, the tears that she was holding back.

He started to reach for her, but Josh was there first, tugging her against his chest, hugging her tight.

Ben wanted to be the one holding her, wanted to be the one who was comforting her.

Wanted...her.

But she wasn't his—or not his alone anyway.

She belonged to Josh, to the team, to herself.

In that moment, though, she belonged to her brother.

So, Ben moved away from them, toward the boxes at the other end of the room, quietly opening them and sorting through the contents.

The words they exchanged were quiet murmurs that he couldn't discern, and though he tried to keep his focus on the task at hand, his gaze went back to Jordyn more than once. She was leaning against Josh, and her brother was wiping her tears away.

After a moment, she sighed, but nodded.

Then her head lifted, her eyes connected with Ben's.

Time stretched, held.

His heart squeezed tight.

She pressed her lips together. Released the plump, kissable mouth that was so damned tempting.

Then tore her gaze from his.

And disappeared into the hall.

Seven

Jordyn

She was sitting in Jess's back yard, beer in her hand, watching the kids run around.

The street in front of the house was filled with cars.

The house was full of people.

There wasn't one box that hadn't been put away—a feat that had taken hardly any time at all. Many hands and all that.

Somewhere along the way, more donuts had appeared (and been devoured), along with a couple of boxes of bagels.

Now, the late afternoon light was beginning to fade, and she was sitting in Jess's yard, watching the chaos, surrounded by people, and...

Thinking that if she could have a life like this then she wouldn't feel so broken.

So much like a failure.

Her sister-in-law, for all intents and purposes, smiled over at her. "Are you overwhelmed or happy?"

"I'm..." She paused as she considered that. "Fine." She smiled. "Though I'm not mom to a newborn, so I think I'm doing a little better."

Jess smiled down at the tiny bundle in her arms, at Jordyn's adorable niece, Amelia, and stroked a hand down her daughter's back. "I do miss sleep."

"It'll get better," she assured, draining the last of her beer, and setting the bottle on the table. "Can I...?"

Jordyn wanted Amelia Time, wanted to snuggle that tiny baby, but Jess hadn't gotten much of an opportunity to hold her daughter since she'd made it over mid-morning, not with all the guys and women taking a turn to get their loving in.

Now, though, she passed Amelia over to Jordyn, who sighed, heart squeezing tight as she cuddled the baby.

Pure bliss.

She loved her boys, loved them so freaking much.

But, God, she wished she had a little girl she could snuggle.

"I'm sorry to steal her from you when you've hardly got any time with her."

Jess sat back in her chair, picked up her own beer, having been convinced it was okay to partake by Nutritionist Rebecca, that, in fact, it could help with milk production. Also, that was truly what the team called poor Rebecca, mostly because there had been two Rebeccas in the organization before PR Rebecca retired and decided to be a full-time mom. Now it was just one Rebecca (though PR Rebecca was still involved in the charity arm of the organization), but the name had stuck.

"I'm used to it," Jess said, referring to the baby thieving. "It's part of the process."

For a team that had each other's backs, it was.

For a woman who'd become increasingly more isolated over the years, it felt...odd. Good but still odd.

Amelia yawned and stretched, latching onto Jordyn's hair, and she started squirming. Jordyn saw the fussiness coming, so she stood and began rocking side to side, that instinctual Mom Rock that had come naturally to her when she'd first become a mom, when she'd spent hour upon hour rocking her fussy, colicky munchkins.

Her boys had been *terrible* babies.

Crying for hours. Needing to be held by her every second of every day. Waking up every hour, day or night.

For three months.

But the moment they hit that threshold, both of them had swung a rapid one-eighty, becoming so easy that she'd almost forgotten about all the crying and sleepless nights.

So much so that her boys were only fourteen months apart.

She'd wanted more kids, but Daniel was done, and she'd always been of the mind that if one half of the couple didn't want more kids, then the whole couple was done.

It was for the best, clearly.

Not just because of her present circumstances, but also because of where they'd been back then.

Daniel had gotten his first of several promotions when Sammy was two months old, and he'd begun traveling.

She'd had a month of two kids under two, one busy, the other needy and not sleeping.

It had been rough, so when Daniel had put her off on discussing the topic of more kids, she hadn't protested. Too fresh.

Later, though, she'd been sad.

"Auntie Jordyn has the best jiggles, doesn't she?" Jess murmured, having found her feet as she rubbed her hand lightly up and down Amelia's back.

"No," Jordyn told her, "it's jiggles *and* Mommy's touch and smell."

"Team effort," Jess agreed.

Amelia's eyes closed with the stroking, and between the two of them, she sank back into sleep.

Though, when Jordyn tried to find her seat again, Amelia got squirmy all over again.

Now *that* was familiar.

Laughing softly, she stood again, rocking and not stopping this time, content to hold her niece and chat with Jess about all things baby, she didn't stop herself from joining in on the conversation when Brit, Mandy, and Anna came over.

They didn't talk about anything important, just about the team's prospects for the season, which was just beginning and then gossip about how long it would take for the single guys to fall, especially with Brit and Mandy determined to play matchmaker (along with most of the married guys).

But all the while, her gaze kept going to the grass where her boys were playing with Mandy's and Anna's kids, Brit's adopted daughter, Roxie, tagging along behind them, trying desperately to do all the big kid things. Coop and Calle had created an obstacle course they were running through, and Jordyn knew that her boys were going to sleep *well* that night.

Her boys, who had convinced Ben to do the obstacle course and were running alongside him, encouraging, trying to help, but mainly just getting in his way.

Sammy so much so that he nearly tripped Ben in his earnestness and almost took all three of them down. Ben didn't get frustrated, not like Daniel would have, he just scooped Samuel up, tossed him over his shoulder in a fireman's hold, and ran through the rest of the course with Sammy bopping up and down.

And the look on Sam's face when Ben put him down.

The gleeful look on Marcus's as he bounced from foot to foot...at least until he set Sammy on his feet. Then Ben was scooping Marcus up, tossing *Marcus* over his shoulder and sprinting through the course.

Giggles filled the air, filled her ears, her belly, her throat.

Her heart rolled over in her chest.

Sammy beelined for Ben the moment he made it back, throwing himself at Ben's legs.

He was tiny compared to Ben, probably couldn't make him stagger back a step, even if he'd put his full force into it, but Ben let Sammy take him down to the grass anyway, let her boys and the other kids try and tickle him into submission.

"Help!" Ben cried. "Save me!"

The giggles intensified and then Mandy's kiddos joined the fray and Roxie sat on Ben's chest and...

It was bedlam and mayhem and—

"Rarrr!" Ben said, sitting up and going on the attack.

She laughed.

How could she not?

She had somehow become part of something so *so* special.

So, yeah, she laughed, and did it loud and free and *her*.

She wasn't making herself small, wasn't trying to keep the boat steady, wasn't trying to be someone else *for* someone else.

She was...happy.

She was content.

She was home.

EIGHT

BEN

He clapped Josh on the back. "I'm out—" He stopped. "You good?"

Josh had just finished a diaper change, if the dirty one folded up next to him on the floor of the living room was any indication.

It was nearing dinner time; most of the guys and their families had gone home.

Okay, *all* of the guys and their families had gone home.

There was no reason for him to have continued to stay.

Except for the fact that he was having a difficult time pulling himself away.

From the boys, from the house, from Jordyn and the warm looks she kept sending his way.

But...Sammy and Marcus had retreated to their rooms, were looking very much like they might not make it to dinner.

They probably wouldn't need it, not with the amount of donuts they'd consumed, not to mention the pizza Brit had ordered in for a late lunch after everything was unpacked. Pizza and garlic bread and salad and—

Yeah, it had been a hell of a Cheat Day.

Now Ben needed to leave them to it.

"I'm good," Josh said, though he was still struggling to tug up the pants on his baby's legs. "She's just so freaking tiny that I can... never..." A grunt. "Freaking get these *on.*" Another grunt. "There," Josh grumbled. "Finally." He picked Amelia up, pressed a kiss to her belly. "Forgive Daddy and his clumsy ass hands." Josh slanted a glance over his shoulder, lips turned up at the edges. "I'm glad you're the one who's watching me struggle. Max wouldn't let me live that last one down."

Ben tapped his chin. "I foresee the nickname Concrete Hands in your future."

Josh had folded the pad he'd been changing Amelia on, and now he straightened, his daughter tucked into the crook of one arm, the pad, wipes, and diaper held in the other hand. "You're lucky that my *Concrete* Hands are full."

Ben snagged the diaper and pad. "Heaven forbid those Concrete Hands drop Amelia."

A glare.

Then a shrug. "Have fun with that diaper."

He'd changed more than enough dirty diapers of his sister's and her kids over the years. A little poop didn't bother him. Hell, he was surrounded by a couple dozen sweaty hockey players, all of whom had various degrees of personal hygiene, on most every day.

So...there was that.

"You heading out?" Josh asked, moving to the table in the hall and snagging the pad from Ben so he could put it and the wipes away.

He *didn't* take the diaper.

Which, as Ben had mentioned, wasn't a problem, even if he knew it was because Josh was trying to fuck with him about the Concrete Hands comment. "Yeah," he said, snagging his jacket off the hook.

"Thanks for your help today."

"No thanks needed."

"Still going to give them to you anyway."

Ben shook his head, but didn't argue, just hit the front door.

"You taking that diaper home as a souvenir?"

He tugged open the panel, stepped out onto the porch. "Gonna toss it in the trash out here." He tilted his head toward the side of the house. "Don't want to stink up her place."

Josh nodded, gave more unneeded thanks.

"Tell Jordyn and the boys bye for me."

A twitch of his lips. "Boys are out, and I don't think Jordyn is far behind."

After he'd closed the door behind him, Ben headed to the trash can, having to reach deep inside to tug out a bag. He didn't want to just toss the poopy diaper loose into the garbage, so he untied the bag, shoved the diaper in, and tied everything up.

Car doors slammed as he lifted the lid and shoved the bag back into the trash.

An engine turned on as he rolled the can back into place, making sure it was behind the fenced-in space for it.

And look at that, the other bins, the recycle and compost ones, were askew. He needed to straighten them, make sure they were tucked neatly away. Who knew if she had an HOA and if it was picky? The last thing she needed was to get a citation on one of her first days.

Rocks crunching as the car backed out of the driveway.

He had to get the trash cans just...*right*.

Also, yes, he was stalling.

And doing it by digging through the trash.

Look at him go.

The engine faded.

The early evening's quiet settled in around him.

Which was when he found himself slipping through the gate, walking softly into the back yard. He made note to put a lock on the latch, so someone couldn't do what he just did and walk into her yard, but it was a faint note, one that was in the back of his mind, because she was standing in the fading sunlight.

And she was beautiful, skin taking on a gilded hint, the flares of light dancing over her hair, her curves.

He wanted her.

He had no right to, not a *single* right to want her, to touch her, to be *here*.

But he was still walking toward her anyway, shifting on silent feet, watching her as she stood there, arms limp at her sides, her head tilting back, eyes going to the sky.

It was easy to see why.

The sunset was fucking beautiful, not nearly as much as her, but it was a sight to see. A band of fog in the distance, and above an ombre of blue to navy, below that stripe of gray and white was red and orange and yellow, a faint glow on the horizon as the sun dipped down, ready to alight on the other side of the globe.

There was a peace to that sky.

One he was hesitant to interrupt.

"I thought you'd gone."

Apparently, he already had.

Or maybe, Jordyn had the same sense he did, the one that drew him to her, that was aware of where she was at all times.

He'd felt that pull from the moment he'd gotten out of his car the night before, felt it in the kitchen, felt it all throughout the day. Every movement, every smile, every laugh, every sip of beer and bite of pizza and hug for her kids, cuddles for her niece...he was aware of *every* single thing she did.

Maybe...she was too?

She certainly turned just as he was within arm's reach, gaze immediately going to his.

And he realized she was waiting for him to reply.

"I couldn't leave," he admitted.

Silence, no more words, just the sound of the breeze in the trees, the last of the birds chirping away, the faint noise of cars in the distance. But, as fucking sappy as it sounded, he could *hear* her, in his eyes, his ears, his heart.

He didn't know this woman.

But he also knew her on every fucking level.

Then she was looking away from him, and it felt like the world had gone quiet, like wool had been shoved into his ears.

"Come on," she whispered.

Full sound. Full color.

Full life.

He followed her up onto the deck to the set of chairs, sitting next to her when she sank into one of them.

She was quiet, but she wasn't silent.

Not when he was finely attuned to the sound of her shifting next to him—the creak of the chair, the soft *shush* of the cushion depressing, the slight scrape of the chair's legs on the deck. He could even track the sound of her breathing, as quiet as it was.

"Why?" she asked.

He managed to tear his gaze from hers. "Don't you feel it, too?"

Her chest, her shoulders rose and fell on a breath, and she went quiet, silent even to his senses that were on high alert, not even breathing, and for long enough that concern began to boil up in his belly.

But just when he was about to tell her to breathe, air hissed out from between her lips.

"I'm not ready."

"I know," he said, even though those three words cut through him. "I know."

But he didn't move, just stayed in that seat next to her, eyes on the sky.

And she didn't move, just stayed in that seat next to him, her eyes on the sky as well.

They sat in that non-silence, no more words exchanged, not even looking at each other as the sun went down, as the night crept in, as the air began to cool, the fog sliding across the sky, masking the stars.

But not masking what he felt deep inside.

And for those couple of hours, just sitting beside her, just *being...*

Ben had never felt less alone.

NINE

JORDYN

She yawned.

And the moment, the quiet, the peace she'd found just sitting next to Ben had disappeared.

"You should go to bed," he ordered softly, his voice a little rough, as though from misuse. And no wonder, they'd been sitting there for long enough that all of her limbs had grown still and slightly numb, that her own voice was rough, too.

"I'm okay."

A brush of his knuckles on her cheek.

She inhaled. That touch...

She wanted more of it.

But...she wasn't ready.

His chair scraped on the deck as he pushed to his feet, reached out his hand. "Come on."

Frozen lungs, stiff legs, tired body and mind and heart. Dinged and dented and...too, too quiet. But she still placed her hand in his, still allowed him to pull her to her feet.

Still let him lead her inside, to the front door.

Only then did he squeeze her fingers lightly, release her hand, and touch her cheek again.

God, how she craved that light bit of contact.

"Go to sleep, sweetpea," he murmured.

Another soft order.

This one she didn't comply with, not completely, anyway. She was going to be walking down the hall, lying down in the master bedroom (sigh), just not before...

"*You* need to go to sleep," she commanded. "You were up later than me."

A flicker in his eyes.

She expected him to get a little testy. Daniel hadn't liked orders.

But it wasn't anger and annoyance in his gaze.

It was warmth.

Like the fact that she'd cared enough to demand that he sleep had touched something inside him.

"Okay, sweetpea," he said.

Sweetpea.

Another piece of him that settled deep in her belly.

Then he was turning away, walking down the driveway, down the street.

She watched him get into his car and pull away from the curb.

And felt like a piece of *her* had gone with him.

———

"Moooom!"

She blinked, eyes flying open, heart instantly in her chest as alertness rocketed through her frame.

Sitting up in a flash, she nearly fell off the couch.

She remembered sitting down there the night before, turning on that crappy movie that Ben had put on for her the night before that.

And that was it.

Her lips turned up into a smile.

Apparently, he'd found a way to cure her insomnia.

Movie on.

Eyes closed.

Brain shut off for—she reached for her cell that was shoved between two cushions, checked the time—twelve hours.

"*Mooom!*"

Thudding feet in the hall, a slender note of worry in Sammy's voice.

It unstuck her, unstuck her voice, her words.

"In here, boys," she called.

Feet coming closer, bedhead galore. Her boys smiling when they saw her, launching into a sprint, jumping into her arms, and knocking her back to the cushions with an "Oof!"

But it was the best sort of way to lose her breath.

Her boys and their little—though not so little anymore—bodies cuddled close, their arms around her neck and torso, squeezing tight.

Her boys were with her.

They were all healthy and safe.

Josh was nearby.

Her adorable niece and Jess were right there with him.

She had a house, had support, had the possibility of new friends, a new support system, and not one that would fuck her husband and decimate her life.

Life had become a clean slate, completely wiped clean.

She got to start over.

How lucky was she?

Before the last couple of days, that was just something she told herself, something she pretended to think, to believe. Bullshit that came from trying to move on.

For her boys.

For herself.

But...on this couch, in this house, with a full night's sleep and the boys in her arms, she could almost believe it.

"Why'd you sleep on the couch, Mommy?" Sammy asked, snuggling close.

She soaked in that *Mommy* since they were coming few and far between nowadays, and usually only in moments like this, in sleepy voices and with her boys faces still creased from sleep. More often she was Mom, and occasionally she was *Bruh.*

But she was doing her level best to nip that last one in the bud.

She'd answer to a lot of things, but *Bruh* was pushing it.

"I fell asleep watching a movie," she told him, smoothing back his hair.

"Your bed would be more comfortable."

She sighed out a laugh, noting the crick in her neck, the stiffness in her lower back. "Yeah," she agreed, "it would have been."

"Can we go to Uncle Josh's for pancakes?"

Now, she laughed for real. "Uncle Josh and Auntie Jess need some time to themselves," she said. "Amelia is little and with both of them traveling for work so much during the season, they don't get a lot of it."

Sammy lifted his head, considered that for long moments. "Like Movie Night?"

She nodded. "Exactly. Uncle Josh and Auntie Jess both work for the hockey team, so during the season they don't have a lot of time for Movie Nights."

"But they came over yesterday," Marcus said. "Did they have time?"

Shit. She hated the thread of worry in his voice.

"They like to spend time with us, too," she reassured him. "And their friends. Plus," she added when his face relaxed, "Auntie Jess and Uncle Josh wanted to make sure we were settled in Auntie Jess's house. You know that thing with the doorknob in the master bedroom?"

Marcus's nodded solemnly. "I thought I was stuck."

"But Auntie Jess showed us how to fix it, right?"

Another nod, this one more like her oldest and less like the unsure little boy of a moment before. "She said I was better at fixing it than even she was."

God, Jordyn loved her sister-in-law.

Joshie had really gotten lucky when he'd found her.

"I'm good at it, too!" Sammy interjected.

"Yes, you are, honey," she said, and sat up, knowing that distraction was going to be in order before this turned into a battle of who was better—her boys were good at turning anything into a competition, even something as innocuous as who could fiddle with the lock on a bedroom doorknob the best. Of course, they'd bicker now about that damn doorknob and then in twenty minutes, they'd be bonding over some YouTuber and calling her *bruh* again.

Which had her lips twitching.

But she smothered her smile, focused on abating the competition, for that moment anyway.

"Now," she said before Marcus could chime in. "I think it's time for pancakes, what do you guys say?"

"With whipped cream?" Sammy asked—or maybe it was a plea.

One that was easy to give in to.

It was easy to give in to homemade whipped cream, fresh berries that she'd spied in her fridge the night before, and Josh's pancake batter recipe. One she'd tweaked just slightly, adding a couple of scoops of plant protein powder, so it would fill up their bellies for a bit longer and be marginally healthier than carb on carb on *carb*—not that she minded the carbs, it was just that her boys were growing and needed good nutrition, not to mention that money was tight, and she needed those bellies to *stay* feeling full.

"And your brekkie potatoes?" Marcus definitely pleaded.

Something that was on the wrong side of healthy considering the amount of butter, but also something that allowed her to sneak in some veggies—peppers and onions sautéed with that butter and lots of garlic, salt, and pepper.

Her mouth watered just thinking about it.

"If we have potatoes," she told him. "Then definitely."

"Yes!" Marcus fist-pumped.

Sammy was, perhaps, more prudent. He jumped off her lap and tore off toward the kitchen. She heard the fridge door open, the contents being jostled, probably as he searched for the whipped cream. Kid had priorities, she thought with a smile. And she couldn't be mad at him for it. The freshly whipped cream was her favorite, too.

Marcus took his younger brother's lead for once and ran into the kitchen, the pantry door crashing into the wall as he flung it open.

She winced.

She would need to pick up some of those circular protectors for the wall, and she should make it a priority, lest Jess end up with holes in every room.

"Mom!"

But that could come later.

"Coming," she called back.

She had lots of things to do that day, not the least of which was registering the boys for school and hitting Target and then she needed to—

She stopped, shook her head, cutting off the mental to-do list.

First...pancakes. Her boys.

That delicious homemade whipped cream with plenty of powdered sugar to sweeten it without turning it liquid.

Fresh berries.

Peppers and onions and plenty of butter and seasonings.

Mornings filled with laughter and love and bickering and competition over doorknobs.

The rest of it could wait.

First came her boys.

TEN

"And then he..." Will was saying a week later. "Get this—he asked if I wanted to go wine tasting at..."

Rome's cheeks went bright red at the statement, and redder when Will told the room the name of the winery. But Ben only caught a glimpse of that scarlet heat before the younger —*so much younger* that he wasn't even twenty-one yet, so he couldn't taste any of that wine he was organizing a tasting of— man bent his head, concentrating very fiercely on tying his skates.

So fiercely that Rome resembled a little kid fumbling through the first time of tying his own laces.

Ben bit back a grin and focused on his own gear.

"Why'd you want to go wine tasting?" Logan asked and his tone was sly. "Were you just gonna smell it?"

"Sneak a sip when the workers' backs were turned?" Kayden didn't hold back his smirk.

Josh's voice was so neutral that it took Ben a moment to tease out the joke. "I heard that he bought a fake ID."

Cackles filled the locker room, and then the shit-giving continued.

But Ben kept quiet.

He knew the reason Rome was so interested in that part of getting dressed.

Being the quiet guy in the locker room often meant that he got to play at being a fly on the wall. Which meant he heard things.

One of those things?

That Rome had the hots for the local winery owner's daughter.

Complicated by the fact that her father worked heavily with the charity arm of the Gold organization...and that same father was closely tied (as in very good friends with) Pierre Barie.

Owner of the Gold.

Fair and a good guy.

But also a scary motherfucker to anyone who dared crossed him. And one could imagine that making a play for his friend's daughter wouldn't exactly be falling in line.

And if Rome broke her heart...

Poor kid.

Ben just hoped he kept his head straight and his cock focused on more appropriate women.

If he dipped his toes in *that* one?

Trouble.

Ben could feel it.

"You know," Coop said quietly. "Calle and I went tasting at that winery. It's the one near the coast, right?"

Uh-oh.

Seemed to be that Ben wasn't the only one who knew Rome's secret.

Then again, the twenty-year-old's mooning was pretty obvious.

Ben got it. The winery owner's daughter, Christina, was beautiful with a rapier wit, but it wasn't her looks that appealed, not even her personality. Rather, there was something warm and bright that seemed to fill the space around her.

He'd only seen it in one other person.

No, he realized as he moved onto his shin guards, he'd seen it in two people.

Mandy...and Jordyn.

Which took his mind somewhere it shouldn't, considering that he needed to focus on the game ahead.

But all he could think of was how her body felt when it was pressed against his—the curves, the soft silk of her skin, the smell of her hair.

How *right* it was.

How *wrong* the fucking timing was.

How much her brother—sitting across the room—would kill *him* if he dared go there.

Winery and team owners, at least, were at a distance. Her *brother* was right in this room, and he was the captain of the team, and he'd helped Ben in ways Ben could never repay. Dating his sister after all Josh had done for him, all he'd done with—

Laughter erupted through the room, shaking him out of his thoughts.

Thank fuck.

He didn't want to think about that now.

They all had a game to focus on, and he only had a three-year contract. If he wanted something longer, if he wanted to stay with the team hopefully until the end of his career, then he needed to prove that he belonged here.

So, he moved quickly through the rest of his equipment, getting dressed in minutes because, thankfully, he'd done this same thing at least a couple of times before. Then he rolled his shoulders, stretched, making certain that everything felt right, was in the proper place.

"How's your sister doing?" Kayden asked Josh as they all started moving to the hall.

"Good," he said. "Got the boys registered for school, and they like their teachers. They're starting soccer next week. Now she's looking for a job, which isn't proving easy, not with being a single parent and childcare hard to find. Ideally, she'd find something that was work from home so that she could still be there for the boys. They're all so close, and I know she'd hate to miss out on school events or games."

Kayden clapped him on the shoulder. "Well, make sure she knows that we're all here for them."

Josh nodded.

Then he was out in the hall.

Ben followed him, trailed him out onto the ice when the time was right, but despite his determination in the locker room to focus on the game and only the game, he was only going through the motions.

His mind was on a woman who glowed with warmth from the inside out, even though that warmth had been stepped on, tamped down, smothered.

His mind was on all the ways he'd be able to get that warmth back, to nurture it so that she felt safe showing it to the world.

His mind was on her scent, her touch, her *boys* who'd brought laughter and smiles to more than a few faces during the barbecue, who brought that same warmth they'd learned from their mother into the world.

His determination had turned to something different.

But he couldn't bring himself to care.

———

"Hey, honey," his mom said the next day.

"How's Maddy?" he asked, taking the bags from her arms, and bringing them into the kitchen.

"Good to see you, too, baby." She rolled her eyes, held still as he bent, kissed her cheek after he'd deposited the bags on the counter. "And only because I know you worry, but your sister is fine."

A tight curl that had been in his belly from the moment she'd called, asking if he was free for a visit, relaxed.

Maddy was never fine.

Not lately.

"Then why are you here?"

She stopped, cocked her head to the side. "Why am I here?" It tilted in the other direction. "Do I need a reason to visit my baby boy?"

No.

But...yes.

He couldn't think of a visit that hadn't been accompanied by him needing to step in, to take over, to carry some extra weight.

He was the man of the house, had been since his father had skipped out on them when Ben was eight years old. That weight was his to shoulder, his burden to bear.

God knew his mom and sister couldn't.

They could barely take care of themselves.

It was fine.

It was...what it was.

She bustled by him, shoulder brushing his arm. "The answer, in case you were wondering"—she poked him in the arm—"is no." A pat now. "I don't need a reason to visit my son."

She might think that...

But history spoke otherwise.

She'd stayed away. She'd created plenty of distance between her and her son after everything had gone down with his sister.

He knew she blamed him and felt guilty for it.

But he didn't hold it against her because...he blamed himself.

The plastic of the bags crinkled as she started pulling things out, shoving them in his fridge. "What are you doing, Mom?"

"Your fridge is pathetically empty," she said. "I noticed it last time I was over." A beat. "And...you might check on your sister, you know."

The last was a whispered addition.

Just snuck in there, a perfectly timed barb.

"I just spoke with her two days ago." Clipped out words.

It had been a nightmare conversation.

As usual.

Plus, his fridge was empty because he was on the road half the time and eating at the rink or practice facility most of the other half. His freezer had some stuff in it, but he rarely ate here at all, especially considering that he was on a strict meal plan. If he had a Cheat Day, he snagged one of the frozen pizzas. If it was a regular diet day, and he happened to find himself here, then he took out one of the glass containers with stuff Nutritionist Rebecca would approve of, slapped it in the microwave, and fueled up that way.

His mom, however, was shoving in all sorts of things he could only eat on a Cheat Day—and no offense to his mom's cooking, but if he was going to have a Cheat Day, then it wasn't going to be with her liquidy tuna casserole and greasy ass spaghetti and meatballs.

He was going to make his Cheat Days count.

"Mom," he began, briefly debating whether it would be easier to let her fill the fridge and then toss it later (a waste) or maybe give the food away (to whom—either it would be another player who couldn't eat it, or their families, who he wouldn't subject his mother's crappy cooking). But he threw that thought out of his head the moment it popped in, knowing that he needed to nip this in the bud.

Right in the bud.

Firm boundaries, that was the only way he knew how to deal with his mother.

"You need nourishment, baby," she said, shoving in another few containers, enough that he would never be able to eat them, even if he wanted.

"Mom," he began again.

"Strength from *my* cooking and not that vegan crap the team wants you to eat." The disdain in the latter half of her sentence speared through him. "Maybe then you'd go visit your sister."

The team that had pulled him from the brink.

The team that had stepped in and helped with just one word from Josh.

The team that had his back from the moment he stepped foot in that locker room.

She was shitting on that, not respecting that.

He snapped.

ELEVEN

JORDYN

Marcus and Sammy loped forward ahead of her, running like the little maniacs they were on the trail.

It was early afternoon, she'd gone home, fed them their after-school snacks, bundled them up into their sweatshirts, strapped them into their booster seats, and had ventured back out.

They needed to do some adventuring.

So, she'd taken them to a trail, not far from their place. It ran behind several clusters of houses, through green space with a lot of old-growth oaks. She'd even caught a glimpse of a creek bed. It had been dry in California, the drought years long, but she still wondered if there was water in it.

The first time she'd driven by on the way to Josh's she'd wanted to explore it.

In all the times since, driving the boys to and fro, that want had turned near obsession.

She *needed* to see what was back there.

And since the boys had come home raring with energy, she'd decided to take them with her—burn off some of that ceaseless vigor, get them away from their screens, and get them all some exercise.

They'd hiked a lot back in Oregon.

It felt good to be doing it again.

That fresh start in action.

"Look at me, Mom!" Sammy called, jumping up on a fallen log and balancing his way across.

"Good job, bud!" she called back, watching him, watching Marcus, but also feeling the damp air on her skin, inhaling the scent of wet earth and trees.

Feeling at home.

At peace.

Yes, this was right.

Smiling when Marcus did a cartwheel in the middle of the trail—and silently thanking the fact that they were alone and no one was in the splash zone of all the particles of dirt he kicked off the bottoms of his shoes as he flipped over—she turned to check where Sammy was.

He'd run even further ahead, was almost disappearing around the corner.

She opened her mouth to call him back, but then he yelled, "Ben!" and sprinted forward, disappearing from her line of sight.

"Crap," she muttered, though her heart began hiccupping in her chest, thudding heavy and fast against her ribs.

Ben.

Ben.

Did she want to see him? Or did she want to run in the other direction?

The answer to that—

Well, she supposed she didn't have a choice either way because Sammy had already disappeared around the corner and Marcus was hot on his brother's trail.

Inhaling deeply, she let the cool, damp air sit in her lungs, her belly...

And then she moved after him, after *them.*

It didn't surprise her that Ben was around the corner, her boys were good with faces, didn't talk to strangers, and were well behaved enough that they didn't run off, unless it was a really good reason.

Though, she supposed, she needed to clarify with them that running after sexy, thoughtful hockey players wasn't a *really good* reason (even if part of her thought it might not be *really* good, but instead it was the *best* reason). But she didn't have time to focus on that, not when she turned the corner after her boys and saw that it was indeed Ben.

Something tightened in her belly.

Her feet slid to a stop.

He had crouched down in front of them, was nodding solemnly as Sammy talked his ear off. Marcus was hopping from foot to foot as he waited for his chance to speak.

"And then Mrs. Hartford closed the book!" Sammy exclaimed. "Right on the last chapter! We're only in first grade," he grumbled. "We hardly ever get to read chapter books."

He made a face that took everything in her to not laugh.

"Yeah, that's because they're *baby books,*" Marcus muttered.

She gasped. "Marcus!"

Ben's gaze shot up to hers, and she had to smother a second gasp.

There was something...deeply wrong in his eyes.

It unsettled her in a place she didn't know existed, filled her with a need to file off, to soften all those jagged edges in him so they didn't jab at him, didn't hurt him, didn't *wound* him.

Because that was what was in his eyes right then.

He looked *wounded.*

"They're not baby books!" Sammy snapped.

Jerking, she glanced at her sons.

"That's enough," she said firmly, and considering she didn't do that particular brand of firm too often, both boys stopped instantly, glancing at her with wide eyes. She held Marcus's. "That was *not* nice," she said, staring him down. "Very *not* nice."

His eyes went glassy.

Sammy's were glassy too.

Shit.

Now she'd gone from fun adventuring to both of her sons being very near tears.

All in front of a big, sexy hockey player who looked at her like—

She shook that off.

Such was the life of a mom.

Smothering a sigh, she turned to Ben. "We interrupted your walk," she murmured. "Feel free to—" A hand covering hers. No. A hand reaching for hers, loosening the fingers she hadn't realized she'd clenched into a fist.

They gently slid between hers, coaxing them apart.

Smoothing them out so they rested on her thigh. Then he glanced at Sammy. "One of my favorite books is *The Monster at the End of This Book,*" he said, his voice even, kind, but that sad was still there. Jordyn could *feel* it. "Have you read it before?"

Sammy shook his head.

"I'll bring it next time." He glanced up at Marcus. "And it's a picture book," he said pointedly, "but I still like it."

Marcus's cheeks went pink.

"But," Ben went on before that pinch of shame turned into a bucketful, "I like chapter books, too."

"Yeah?"

Ben nodded then leaned a little closer. "But want to know what my secret is?"

Marcus froze, but then because he was never a kid to resist curiosity, he nodded.

"I'm working on building the Lego Millennium Falcon."

Her son gaped. Books might be his favorite, but never let it be said that he hadn't been bit by the Lego bug too. "B-but that's got like six thousand pieces!"

"Seven thousand five hundred," Sammy said solemnly, awe in each word.

"Whoa."

"Yeah," Ben murmured. "And it's taking me forever."

"I can help," Marcus said quickly, the pink gone, excitement in him again as he bounced from foot to foot. "I'm really good at Legos!"

"Are you?"

Sammy. Her sweet boy, Sammy, could have taken the chance to be a jerk to his brother, especially because Legos were "his thing." Instead, he was sweet and said, "He is. Marcus is really good at building Legos."

"Then I think I'd be lucky for him to help me. What do you say, Marcus?"

Her oldest nodded. "Yes," he said, the agreement so quick, it was barely discernible.

Ben put out a fist for them each to bump. "Well, then"—he stood up—"we have a plan. You'll help me with the Falcon."

"Can I help, too?"

She waited for Marcus to snap back, to show that mean streak of his father's, the one that had been appearing more and more often of late, the one that had her worried he was going to turn out like Daniel.

It was a fear that jabbed at her at regular intervals.

Fresh start, but the old demons still lurked in the shadows.

But before she could encourage the conversation in the direction that wouldn't point right back to tears, Marcus said, "Yeah." He glanced at Ben. "Sammy is good at Legos, too. They're his favorite thing *ever*."

Relief poured through her.

That was her son.

That was her baby.

Not the angry glimpses of his father that he'd been showing.

Not the picking and mean comments.

Marcus was kind and sweet and one of her favorite people in the whole wide world.

"Marcus taught me how," Sammy said quickly. "I'm really

good with the little pieces." He held up a hand, waggled the digits. "That's because I have little fingers."

"He is." Marcus moved to the edge of the trail, was climbing on another fallen log. "He is really good with the little pieces."

Now those were her *babies.*

Those were the men she was trying to raise—strong, yes, but kind.

Kind of like the man in front of her, the one who'd settled the argument (without UNO, no less), who'd soothed egos and prevented tears.

The man with the hurt in his hazel eyes, a cool metallic tang added to the mixture of warm brown and gold and green.

But that cool didn't penetrate the conversation with her boys. Instead, Ben smiled and put up his own hand, and God, it was *huge* compared to hers, to Marcus's, to Sammy's. "You do. See?" He bent, held it up.

Sammy pressed his palm to Ben's. "Whoa."

Ben grinned and then she was the one at risk of tears. Luckily, she had plenty of experience holding them back and managed just in time to watch Ben's grin widen when Sammy tore off after Marcus, the two of them leaping from log to log. There was a big pile of logs that had apparently been left behind from some tree trimming work.

Nirvana for her sons.

And a plus that her boys weren't destroying the trail.

A mom had to take her victories as they came, no matter their size.

She followed after them and when Ben moved beside her, she glanced up at him. "You don't have to let us disturb your walk."

Silence, but just for a moment. "I don't mind."

The boys' chatter sounded in the distance, the happiness and excitement evident, and mostly from the man next to her.

Maybe that was why she asked what she did.

"Will you tell me why you hurt?"

TWELVE

BEN

*W*ill you tell me why you hurt?

Ben nearly tripped over his own feet.

Hockey skills saved him.

He took a breath, made sure he didn't end up on his ass, and then turned to face her. "Why do you think I'm hurt?"

Silence.

A long moment of quiet that filled the space between them, that brought the noise of her boys into the forefront of his mind.

So carefree and happy...even though their life had imploded.

Because of the woman next to him.

Because she'd made it her mission to make sure that change didn't touch her kids.

And his mother—

She hadn't done that.

She *couldn't* do that.

His mother didn't have that instinct.

It was part of why his sister was so fucked up.

Jordyn's hand came to his arm, drawing him to a stop about twenty feet from her boys, who were now picking up the logs, looking for any critters that might be living beneath them. He was going to warn them to be careful of snakes or spiders or whatever dangerous critters might be beneath them (rattlesnakes, black widows, brown recluses), but then she stepped in front of him, took his hand in hers, and whispered, "I can see the hurt in your eyes."

He blinked, shielding his expression, breaking the connection.

Hiding that hurt.

Because...she couldn't see it.

Because he couldn't allow her to see it.

"I'm fine," he said.

Was it terse?

Fuck yes, it was.

But *she couldn't see it.*

That silence—punctuated only by her boys playing—dropped over him like a ton of bricks. It hurt, *hurt*...because he could see that the terse hurt *her*.

Asshole.

"Right," she whispered.

And she started to turn away, to move back to her boys, to leave him and—

Every cell in his body revolted at that thought, every muscle tensed, and the word was torn from him. "Wait."

She stopped, rotated back to face him, brows up, eyes searching.

He tried to hold tight to the mask, tried to pretend nothing was bothering him.

But she saw through it anyway.

Her fingers found his again, squeezed lightly. "You don't have to tell me," she said softly. "I swear, it's not a trick question." Her hand fell away and he hated that she wasn't touching him, that she was drawing away. "I'm just..." Quiet for another few heartbeats. "I'm just...here, okay?"

He touched her cheek. "I know."

God, how could her skin be that soft, how could she be so delicate?

He could hurt her, physically, he could seriously hurt her, but what was worst was that he knew he could hurt her emotionally, that he could do it so easily, and *that* was the thing that gave him pause, the thing that was tearing him up inside.

He didn't want to hurt her.

"I'm fine."

Her eyes flickered. "Okay," she murmured, sliding back a step.

His gut twisted...and he realized that he *was* hurting her.

By cramming it all inside, by shoving it down and locking her out.

Worse, he realized that she was at a disadvantage.

He knew what hurt her. He knew that bad history. He knew why she'd moved down here, what had gone down with her ex.

She was an open book.

And if he couldn't be open with her in return...

It shouldn't matter. They barely knew each other. They hadn't made any promises, made any ties—except the last was a lie. There was a connection between them. Even just standing there on a quiet trail, her boys in the distance, the possibility of someone walking by, and it was like the universe had just been reduced to her, to her family, to him. There was a steel rope tying them together, an anchor in his chest that made it so he couldn't free himself.

Maybe he should be worried that he didn't *want* to free himself.

But all he knew was that he wanted to foster that connection, to add to the steel, to tie her to him in the same way.

Which meant that he needed to be open with her.

"I *am* upset."

Fuck, he felt like an idiot just admitting that, but watching her response gave him the confidence to go on. Just those three words had her expression softening and she shifted back, moving to his side, pressing her body to his.

Those fingers brushing his again. "Why, honey?"

A breath, claws tearing up the back of his throat, making the words stick, but he breathed through them. "I snapped at my mom."

Her face gentled further. "What happened?"

Another breath, trying to release those claws, but fuck, explaining why he'd snapped would mean explaining so much more than why a single conversation had gone off the rails.

"You don't have to tell me any more," she told him, soft and warm and—

"It's not you," he said. "It's just...complicated."

"You and your mom, or the conversation?"

"Both," he admitted. "My dad left when I was little and my mom..." What was the most innocuous way to describe it? "My mom didn't handle it well."

Her fingers found his, holding tight, but she didn't push for more. She just held his hand and waited.

And that patience unlocked him.

"That's not true," he whispered. "She didn't just not handle it. She fucking went off the rails. She didn't take care of me, didn't take care of my sister, didn't take care of the house." A sigh. "I was too little to know how to do it, but I figured it out the best I could, at least with the house stuff. My sister..."

God, his sister was such a struggle.

She'd been attached to his hip, had clung tight to him.

Until he'd left her.

For that, she'd never forgiven him.

And now—

A scream pierced through the air.

It was loud enough that any thought of his past, his mom and his sister were rent from his brain, and he was moving in an instant, instinct taking him to the logs, to Jordyn's boys.

Marcus was standing beside the pile, frozen, his hands at his side.

And Sammy—

His heart thudded hard.

Blood was dripping down his face, his shirt, and his arm...his arm wasn't quite right. It was hanging weird and—

He screamed again.

"Fuck," Ben whispered, stepping over the logs, moving toward Sammy and scooping him up. The inhuman and pained sound that came out of Sammy's lips when Ben lifted him would sit like a wound in his heart forever, it was that awful.

But he had to get him out of the logs.

"Sammy!" Jordyn was right by his side.

"Support his arm," he ordered, and though he probably shouldn't be giving orders, he knew that Sammy's arm dangling was hurting him, and Ben couldn't hold him and his arm.

Thankfully, Jordyn didn't bristle.

She just carefully put her hands on Sammy's arm, tucking it in against his body and holding it so that it didn't bounce around.

She was incredibly gentle, but Sammy still made another one of those inhuman noises.

When her eyes hit his, he knew it pained her as much as it did him. No. More, of course, since she was his mother. It was just... this boy was already in Ben's heart. Goofing around at the barbecue. Being sweet to his brother on the trail. Bringing warmth to his mother's face.

"Where are you parked?" he asked.

"At the parking lot near the trailhead." She glanced at Marcus. "Come on, honey."

Her tone was calm and steady, but he could see the panic and terror in her eyes.

"My house is closer," he said, nodding toward the opposite side of the creek. "That's my back yard. We just have to go across the bridge right there." He inclined his head to the little wooden-planked bridge. "Let's take him inside, clean him up, and splint that arm."

Her throat worked. "Okay. Marcus, baby, do you see the bridge?"

"Y-yes."

He was terrified, too.

"Marcus?" Ben asked.

The boy looked up at him.

"My keys are in my pocket"—he nodded to his left pocket—"can you grab them out for us, bud?"

Still frozen.

Damn.

"Bud." A bit sharper now, but only so much as to draw him out of the ice.

Marcus blinked.

"Keys, buddy, okay?"

He tugged the keys out of Ben's pocket.

"You're on door duty." He glanced at Jordyn. "You're next to me, holding this arm." A look slanted down at Sammy. "And you're just going to hang on, bud, okay?"

Sammy had gone still. Too still for the busy little boy.

Ben had to get moving.

"It'll be okay," Ben told them. "Let's go now."

Then he was walking carefully forward, Marcus gripping the keys tightly, Jordyn at his side. He hated that he was jostling Sammy, that he was hurting him.

But he had to get Sammy to his house.

And then, based on the pain and the way his arm was hanging, Ben needed to get Sammy to the hospital.

THIRTEEN

JORDYN

"Help him with the lock, sweetpea."

Another soft order.

And she shook herself, carefully releasing Sammy's arm, and moving to help Marcus with the lock. Ben had already directed him to the right key, she realized. Her boy was just struggling to turn it.

She moved forward quickly, and as she did so, she mentally slapped herself.

She was the boys' *mom*.

She needed to get her shit together.

A second later, the door was open, and they were walking into a spacious kitchen, a large living room just beyond it. She stepped to the side, letting Ben lead, taking a second to lock up behind him.

By the time she made it into the living room, Ben was laying Sammy on the couch, getting Marcus to help him shift the pillows to support Sammy's arm.

"Your couch," she whispered. "The blood—"

There was absolutely no room for negotiation in his tone. "It doesn't matter."

So she left it, turning back to the kitchen, grabbing a roll of paper towels, wetting several to clean the blood from Sammy's face and arm.

"Thanks, buddy," Ben was telling Marcus when she made it back over to him. "Now, can you go down the hall? My bedroom is at the end of it." Marcus nodded, skin still pale, but the panic having faded with having been given a series of tasks. "Go into my closet and grab a couple of ties from the rack, okay? It doesn't matter which ones."

Marcus took off.

"Hey, honey," she whispered to Sammy, gently wiping the blood away from his face. He had a couple of scratches, the remnants of a bloody nose, and a split lip. But none of those would require a doctor, except maybe for an antibiotic.

His arm though.

That...scared her.

He cried out *every* single time it was jostled, and fuck, she would never be able to forget the sound of his pain, not for the rest of her life.

She grabbed a thin pillow just as Marcus came out from the hall, and the next couple of minutes were hell.

Pillow beneath his arm, ties used to hold it in place.

Sounded simple...it wasn't.

Not when it was *her* baby in pain.

Not when it was *her* causing him pain by securing his arm.

Maybe she should have called an ambulance, made them do it, but she had no clue how long the response time would be, how long Sammy might be left waiting. At home, it would have taken ages. Here...they were closer to civilization, so maybe it was the wrong call—

"Car keys are hanging on the hooks in the kitchen, bud. Can you grab them for me?"

Marcus zipped into the kitchen.

Ben glanced at her. "Ready?"

She was sweating, was near tears, but she needed to get her boy to the hospital, so she locked it down, braced his arm when Ben stood, and then the three of them were walking slowly through the kitchen, navigating the couple of steps down into the garbage.

"Into the back, bud," Ben told Marcus, who scrambled over the middle seat, leaving footprints on the leather before he began buckling into the back seat.

Ben didn't skip a beat.

Didn't freak about the footprints.

Just looked at her and said, "You next, sweetpea."

She somehow made her way inside still supporting Sammy's arm and Ben bent as he set him carefully on the seat. A few moments later, they were strapped in, the door was, closed, and Ben was in the driver's seat.

"I don't know where the hospital is," she said softly.

She hadn't found a pediatrician for the boys yet, hadn't searched up hospitals. She'd been too busy getting everything else sorted.

Hell, she should have known her littlest would have made the hospital a priority.

He was always hurting himself.

But not like this.

Ben's gaze hit hers for a beat before it pointed out the rear window and he continued backing up onto the street. "Don't worry, sweetpea. I do."

There was...a lot in those words, in the glimpse of his eyes.

He'd spent time at that hospital, maybe so much that he could make the drive with his eyes shut.

Hockey was a rough sport—no doubt he'd had his share of injuries—but she didn't think that was why he knew where the closest hospital was, didn't think him playing a sport that was dangerous and intense and brutally physical at times was responsible.

But she couldn't focus on it right at that moment.

She smoothed back Sammy's hair, talked softly to both of her boys, reassuring them that it would be okay.

And then they were pulling into the hospital and she and Ben were getting Sammy out of the SUV.

Inside the hospital, Marcus trailing them.

Ben sitting with her boys while she checked in at the counter.

And it wasn't until she was showing her insurance card, thanking fuck that Daniel had agreed to keep the boys on it until she got a job, that she realized this was different.

This was different.

Not because of Daniel's insurance, as brittlely thankful for it as she was.

But because she hadn't been alone, because her boys hadn't been alone.

Not for one second had she felt like she was navigating this by herself.

Ben.

Her eyes hit his as she went to them with the assurances that they would be taken back right away, and she felt the truth like a punch in her gut.

He'd been there for her more over the course of a couple of weeks than Daniel had been there for her in...well...

Ever.

Something else to consider.

Later.

Because now she needed to be with her boys.

But part of her couldn't help but think that Ben had just slotted himself in right long aside Marcus and Samuel.

That her two boys had become three.

It was past dinnertime when they finally made it back to her house.

She was exhausted, and she still had to get her car and make something for them to eat.

Sammy...he'd been a champ.

He'd broken both bones in his arm, had needed to be sedated for them to reset them, and was currently sporting a brace that didn't appear to be doing *anything*.

But Sammy had pain meds and was much more comfortable now that everything was back in place.

He was also queasy, so dinner would probably be something small and simple.

She reached for the front door, keys out, ready to jam the proper one into the lock, when it swung open.

Josh was there, face filled with concern, Jess and Amelia behind him.

For a moment, she blinked in confusion.

"I called them," Ben said, moving up behind her, carrying Sammy since he was still feeling a little shaky, or wanted comfort, or...just wanted Ben.

Something else Ben hadn't blinked at, hadn't hesitated over.

He'd just carefully helped Sammy from the car, cradled him against his chest.

Jordyn's heart squeezed.

"We grabbed your car," Jess said. "Josh parked it in the garage."

"Thanks," she whispered, stepping to the side so that Ben, Sammy, and Marcus could go inside.

"I knew you'd want him," Ben murmured, hesitating on the threshold, their gazes connecting. "And I knew he'd want to be here for you."

Her heart squeezed again.

"Thanks." Another whisper.

"No worries, sweetpea."

Then he was inside.

Josh reached for her the moment she'd come close, Marcus

already in his arms, and hugged her tight enough that she finally felt like she could take a deep breath.

She'd had to help hold Sammy down while the doctors had set his breaks.

He'd been medicated, sedated, but he'd still screamed and struggled and—

More marks on her soul, more things she wouldn't ever be able to get out of her head.

Marcus squirmed, so Josh let him down. "Jess cooked dinner for you, bud, you want to head into the kitchen?"

Never one to miss a meal, and no doubt starving after the long hours in the ER's waiting room (Ben had offered to take him home, but he'd refused to leave his brother), not to mention probably looking for a slice of normalcy, Marcus beelined it for the kitchen.

Josh dropped both of his hands on her shoulders. "You good?"

"Yeah," she whispered. "It was dumb luck that we ran into each on the trail. If he hadn't been there…"

She sucked in a breath, released it slowly.

Josh's hands tightened.

"I would have been okay." She gave him a rueful smile. "God knows, I've done it on my own plenty of times in the past."

His hands loosened and he shifted, sliding his arm around her shoulders. "I know you would have been okay, honey. But"—he led her down the hall into the kitchen and she didn't miss his gaze going to Ben, who was carefully setting Sammy in a chair—"I'm glad you weren't on your own."

Ben ruffled Sammy's hair then turned and did the same to Marcus.

Her heart did that thing again.

And she couldn't deny that she wanted it to *keep* doing it.

To maybe do it forever.

FOURTEEN

BEN

He sucked in the cool air coming up off the ice, felt the way it tightened the skin inside his nose, how it settled in the back of his throat, his belly.

His fingertips tingled.

His pulse was already increasing.

His legs shook, as they always did before every game, just a little bit.

He bounced off his toes, the black rubber skate mat beneath his feet, waiting for the music to start, for the guys in front of him to move, to get on the ice.

Time to fucking go.

Or at least when the music started.

Grinning, he rolled his shoulders, bounced on his skates, impatiently waiting. And he wasn't alone. The hall was filled with a line of pumped, excited players, all ready to get on the fucking ice.

But it would be a hurry up and wait scenario.

Hurry up onto the ice, skate a couple of laps, go to the bench. Wait. For the national anthem (or anthems, if they were playing a

Canadian team). Wait some more if there was a ceremonial puck drop or presentation. Then finally *go.*

Except, he had to wait for his turn on the ice.

Then he finally got to go...at least for a good forty-five seconds. Then he had to haul his ass back to the bench...to wait.

He smothered a grin, knowing it would ruin his badass image.

Not so much.

But it was game time.

He needed to focus.

Thankfully, the game song came on at that moment and the guys started moving so he didn't need to think about waiting or focusing.

And thankfully, it was just one anthem, no special puck drops, no jerseys being retired.

Then game time.

The puck hit the ice; the guys sprang into motion.

He watched, eyes glued to the game, focusing on all the little details. That was part of why he'd made it this far. He was big, but not huge. He was fast, but not the fastest. He had decent hands, but not great ones. There was nothing very much special about him (hence the reason it had taken him so fucking long to get to this point). The biggest thing he had going for him was his hockey sense.

He used his brain.

He focused on the little details.

And he had the determination to claw his way here.

So, his gaze was glued to the ice, following the players, looking for openings, for breakdowns on both his side of the ice and on his opponent's.

Then he exploited or fixed to the best of his abilities, depending on what he spied.

There—that defenseman was playing aggressively, pinching and high up on the ice. If the right opportunity presented itself, they could get an odd man rush or a breakaway.

There was an opportunity to exploit the weak side—one of their guys was open in the front of the net in the offensive zone.

There was space to make a pass.

There was the moment to move fast, to not sit on the puck, to get it up the ice to his teammates.

There was his change.

And then it was less about thinking and more about trusting his body to put all that *thinking* to good use.

It was time to play some fucking *hockey.*

His skates hit the ice and he was in motion, sprinting to his wing on the far side of the ice, challenging the opposing player who was skating in with the puck, pushing him to the outside so fuck if his opponent would be able to get the pass off—or at the very least, if he did manage to make it, he wouldn't be able to get a *good* pass off.

That was what happened then.

Ben skated his ass off and angled his body, and—*ha!*—the fucker *did* try to make the pass. It ricocheted off his shin guards, bounced into the corner, where Logan easily picked it up and swept it to the other side of the ice.

And just like that, Ben was sprinting again, flying up the ice and joining in on the rush.

He received a pass at the top of the circles, got slashed for his troubles, but managed to chip it deep, to give his teammates time and space to set up as he chased it down.

His breath whooshed out of him as he was checked into the boards, but he didn't lose the puck, and when he managed to chip it over to Rome, he sucked in a breath, took off for the net.

Will was there already, battling for position in front of the opposing goalie.

The puck slid from the corner, pushed out by Rome.

Will reached for it, pulled it back, shot, and...

The goalie grabbed it.

Hell.

But it was time to change, time to go wait again, and they'd had a good shift. Good enough that he accepted the fist bumps once he'd sat down, good enough that he let Calle's thump on his shoulder sink in, to fuel him.

Good enough that he risked *one* glance to the box overhead.

He could see people in the team's luxury box, but he didn't allow himself to look long enough, didn't want to risk looking, seeing, being drawn in.

It had been a week since Sammy broke his arm.

He'd gone over for dinner twice...well he'd *brought* dinner— and some Legos, though he hadn't schlepped over the entire Falcon, not wanting to bring something that would be difficult for Sammy to participate in, especially since building Legos was his favorite thing in the whole wide world.

And each time, he'd hung around while Jordyn put the kids to bed. Ostensibly doing the dishes, but mostly drawing that task out so that he could hang out after they fell asleep.

Could tempt Jordyn onto the couch.

Could find out that she liked a cup of tea in the evenings now that it had gotten cold. With plenty of honey, and to sit bundled up on the back deck, enjoying the quiet of the night.

He liked making that for her.

He liked being the one who brought it to her.

He liked sitting next to her on the wicker love seat, waiting until she got tired enough to slump against him, so he could feel her curves pressed to his body, smell her shampoo, hear her soft recap of the day.

They were...

Not talking about what they were.

Since that day—since he'd asked her for her number in the ER waiting room so they could keep in touch as Sammy was treated —they'd texted every day.

They were...

Still not talking about what they were.

But he knew that she was someone important, someone he

couldn't go more than a few hours (if he was lucky) without thinking about her.

And, for now, for the woman in the box that night, the woman who wasn't ready for more, that was enough for him.

His change came hurtling toward the bench and Ben stood up, hopped over the board, and landed on the ice.

Back to work.

Back to playing smarter not harder.

Back to burning lungs and quads and ass. Back to sucking wind and trying to eke out one more stride that would put him in front of the players on the other team. Back to crushing hits into the boards. Back to battling for an inch, a tip of the puck, a shot on net.

Back to *hockey*.

But even as he used his brain, used his sense, used *all* his focus for that.

Jordyn was still in the back of his mind.

FIFTEEN

JORDYN

A cast didn't stop Sammy.

Not in the least.

Hell, she almost thought it gave him a super boost. One arm was securely encased in padding and fiberglass.

He could run, he could jump, he could do *anything!*

And not hurt that arm.

Oh, to have his stamina, healing ability, or pain tolerance.

She was still aching from having stubbed her toe that morning.

Getting ready for a job interview that had...gone horribly. So horribly she'd wanted to bolt out of the office almost from the moment she'd sat down, but also it was the only bite she'd gotten on her resumé submissions since she'd moved down here.

Which meant that she might have to take it anyway.

And to have to work under that boss, the one who'd stared too long at her breasts and then made it clear that her hours didn't begin at nine and end at five—but that she needed to be on and available throughout all hours of the day *and* the weekends— would be freaking unbearable.

She'd been here for her boys from the moment they'd grown in her belly.

To miss out on them for more than normal working hours would slowly kill her.

She couldn't.

Couldn't.

But she might have to.

Daniel was being...

Well, he was ready to let her go, let their boys go.

She'd go to court. She'd make fucking sure that her boys had what they needed, what Daniel was obligated to give to them.

But that wouldn't be easy if he cut them off, if he took them off the insurance.

Like he'd threatened to do the night before.

Because he'd gotten the explanation of benefits in the mail, along with a bill.

She'd paid the copay in the ER, tried to make sure they'd send the bill to her new place, but wires had been crossed or someone hadn't followed through, and the bill had been sent to her old house, or well, to *Daniel's* house.

He'd been...apoplectic.

And she wouldn't put it past him to turn threats into reality.

He'd done it before, after all, turned that affair into a separation into a divorce where he drove her far away, shoved off all his responsibilities, and got to keep fucking her former best friend.

All of which meant that she needed to tread carefully, especially with Sammy's arm.

She needed to not rock the boat. She needed that insurance in place for his follow-up appointments and care.

She needed to find her own job for her own insurance.

So, boob-staring, work-all-hours-of-the-day boss might be her only hope.

Sigh.

Maybe another resumé refresh was in order.

She could dress up stay-at-home mom as...chief home officer?

Family manager? Project coordinator for extremely tricky and oftentimes testy clients?

Chief tantrum manager?

Poopy diaper extraordinaire?

That last had her smothering a smile. It had been years since she'd changed a diaper—well, not counting Amelia's that she'd changed that evening.

It was her, Amelia, Marcus, and Samuel—and a gaggle of other wives and girlfriends and kiddos—but she'd sprung her niece from the babysitter, gathered all the various accoutrements for two kids, one baby, and a broken arm, and had accepted Josh's invitation to the game.

Now they were in the owner's box high above the arena, watching the guys play below, but the majority of her things were down the hall in the Family Suite.

At the ready.

Along with all of the activities that had been cooked up for the kiddos that night.

The theme was apparently glitter, heaven help them all.

Crafter's herpes would certainly be making a home in *her* home.

But for the moment, she was safe from the sparkly terror. Because her boys were entranced. They'd watched a couple of games before, but when they were younger, and it hadn't been all that fun for any of them, not when she'd spent the whole time wrangling and they'd spent the whole time whining about wanting to run up and down the stairs.

Tonight, though, they were in love.

And she couldn't blame them.

Being up in the box meant they had a hell of a view—no tall people in front of them blocking parts of the ice, no having to squint because they were in the nosebleeds, no pesky people getting up and down at regular intervals.

Just them, some of the support staff, and a few of the higher-ups (*eek*). The last was something she'd given her boys the Mom

Talk about before they'd entered—behave, don't get in the way of people doing their work, be quiet, be respectful, don't run, sit in their seats, don't bang their cast against anything, least of all anything breakable.

The usual.

Of course, she'd watched their eyes glaze over at *behave,* so who knew how successful her Mom Talk would be.

Especially when she was jiggling a newborn.

For the moment, though, all was going fine. Her boys were in chairs and completely focused on the game. She and Amelia were jiggling off to the side so as not to block anyone's view.

And the Gold were kicking butt down below.

No goals yet, but they were dominating, spending most of the time in the offensive zone.

A lot of that was due to one of their newer players—or she guessed, he wasn't *new,* exactly. He'd been moved up from the Gold's AHL team, the Rush, invited to play a few games to see if he could hang at this level. Or maybe to just fill an empty roster spot? Or...well, she didn't know all of the idiosyncrasies. He was there that night, and according to her watchful eye (take it for what it was worth from her experience as a sister of an NHLer), he should be there permanently.

Axel Finnegan was kicking some serious *ass.*

Sammy sat up straighter.

Marcus jumped to his feet. "Oh...yes!"

His cheer joined in with the rest of the arena as the Gold, as Axel Finnegan, scored, and it was a pretty one. Pretty enough that with her hockey sister knowledge, she immediately looked to the Jumbotron, eyes glued to the replay.

"That was *lit,*" Sammy breathed, jumping up and down, both arms in the air (one rather more successfully than the other, considering the cast prevented full extension).

Marcus was whooping as he jumped up and down and Jordyn's heart squeezed hard.

Again. Like it had so many times in the few weeks she'd been living here.

This was...living.

This was so much more than she'd had back home.

She couldn't yet say that she was thankful for the way that Daniel imploded their family, but she *was* thankful to be here, to be with her brother and the family he'd made, thankful to be able to hold her niece and watch her boys cheer their heads off.

Thankful for...Ben.

She barely let herself think the last.

It was a dangerous thought. And she'd meant it when she said she wasn't ready for a relationship, and she wouldn't ever treat Ben like he wasn't worth more than exploring the attraction she felt with him.

But she *was* attracted to him—there was no denying that she wanted him.

It had been so long since she'd been with a man, and she'd never wanted one like she wanted Ben.

And there was a certain freedom in allowing herself to feel that.

A freedom in her feelings, in what she permitted herself to notice, to acknowledge, to tuck close to her heart.

She wanted to fuck Ben's brains out.

There.

She'd said it...or rather, she'd thought it.

And she didn't burst into flames or spontaneously combust.

She was just here with her happy boys, holding her happy niece, her eyes on her brother—and Ben—down below.

That was okay.

It was okay to want him.

But...was it okay to want him for more than fucking when she'd spent her life tied to Daniel, when she'd made promises to herself, to her boys that she would build something for them?

Something *good.*

Would any of that, any of her work at all that building mean anything if she tied herself to another man so soon?

Would that make her weak?

Codependent?

Would—

She bit back a sigh as Ben's face appeared on the Jumbotron and her heart did that squiggle squaggle again.

Because, really, did any of these questions even matter if the ties to Ben had already been formed?

Her eyes slid to the bench, immediately found number thirty-eight.

Ben's number.

And she had a feeling that it didn't.

That fate had already decided.

SIXTEEN

BEN

The game had gone well.

Really well, actually.

They'd beaten the Sierra handily, and that hadn't been a guarantee. The Sierra were a tough matchup, even though the newest team in the league was, just that, new and new teams tended to be easy pickings as they filled out their rosters the first couple of seasons.

The Sierra were different.

They'd come into their inaugural season raring, feet firmly on the gas pedal, and they hadn't stopped.

Today, though, the Gold had come out on top.

And it felt fucking great.

He'd never get over the feeling of winning.

The buzzer going off, knowing they'd gotten the two points?

Yeah, they might all pretend that it was fine when they lost, that they just needed to refocus and look forward. But losing really fucking sucked, even when he was supposed to be professional about it.

Losing to the Sierra, who were quickly becoming their newest and strongest rivals, would sting like a motherfucker.

Luckily, they didn't have to deal with any of that tonight.

Tonight it was just the glory of that win, the joy that came from pulling out a good game, and sundaes from the Dairy with Jordyn and the boys coming up as soon as he got dressed. Maybe he could sneak her away, could get a few moments with just the two of them. He couldn't kiss her, though he'd been thinking of it, dreaming of it, *planning* it.

Not until she was ready.

But maybe she'd let him hold her for a little bit.

"What's the hurry?" Josh asked on his way back to his locker.

Ben was tugging on his socks but froze at the question, feeling suddenly tongue-tied. Mostly because he'd been thinking about Josh's sister, thinking about kissing her, about feeling that curvy body of hers against his.

Now he cleared his throat.

Forced himself to hold Josh's eyes. "I'm taking the boys and Jordyn out for ice cream at the Dairy."

It was Saturday night.

No school the next day.

No schedules pummeled.

Just her and him and the boys.

Josh went still for a long moment. Then his brows lifted. "You've been spending a lot of time with my sister."

A quiet comment, but Ben didn't miss the warning laced through every word.

If he hurt Jordyn, Josh would eviscerate him.

He'd deserve it.

Jordyn was...

Something he couldn't focus on, not right at that moment with Josh staring him down like he was the worst sort of scum.

So he didn't bother lying. "I like her a lot." A breath. "I like them all a lot. She and her boys are great."

Josh's chest rose and fell on an inhale and exhale. "They *are* great."

And the implication beneath that statement being that if Ben fucked up that *great* in even the slightest way that he'd be worse than scum, worse than eviscerated.

Worse than dead.

Which was why he gave Josh the truth for a second time. "She's not ready."

Josh's brows lifted.

"I-I—she's *not* ready," he said again. "And I respect that. But she's here starting over, and the boys are awesome and she's... *great.*"

Not poetry.

Far from it.

But it was honest, and he was staring up at her brother, and that was all he could be.

"I haven't forgotten what you did for me," he said. "I haven't forgotten what you did for my sister. I wouldn't—I *won't* treat yours with anything but respect. Not only because she deserves better."

Silence.

Josh's intense gaze fixing Ben in place.

Long enough that his lungs began to feel tight, that he wondered if he'd truly fucked this all up by being honest.

Laughter echoed through the room, Brit's distinctive amusement filling the air.

Josh unfroze.

Or maybe that was just wishful thinking.

"I won't say go easy with her because she can handle herself." Josh's jaw clenched. "But I will warn you to go slow because if you hurt her..."

The threat didn't get finished.

Because it didn't *need* to get finished.

Ben had already heard the unspoken words loud and clear.

• • •

The elevator doors dinged as they opened and he stepped out into the hall, turning toward the faint hum of noise.

He'd been up here, up to the Family Suite, a time or two but only to pass along a message that someone would be running late, usually Brit and usually Brit because she'd been pulled into some extra press.

That had ramped up increasingly recently, this being what was probably her last season.

Everyone wanted a sound bite, a chance to interview her.

But tonight he wasn't there for Brit.

He was there to see Jordyn, Marcus, and Sammy.

The din increased as he approached the door, the volume turning into an ear-buzzing cacophony as he pushed through.

Filled with people.

Filled with activity.

But his gaze arrowed straight toward Jordyn's.

She was talking animatedly with Stefen—former Gold captain, though he now joked that he liked to be referred to only as Brit Plantain's husband—her hands gesturing widely as she spoke. Stefen was grinning as she talked.

Ben quietly closed the door behind him. Not that anyone would have heard it, even if it slammed.

Sammy was constructing a tower out of wooden blocks, his cast not stopping him in the least from building it so high, he was already lifted on tiptoe, just so he could place the latest block.

Marcus was lying on a big pillow in the corner, reading a book.

Everything in him *settled.*

Like he was home.

Finally, he was home.

Then Jordyn glanced up and her face shone with that warmth that lit her from the inside out, and he knew.

Knew.

She was it for him.

· · ·

"Oh God, that peanut butter chocolate bowl is my favorite," Jordyn said, flopping back onto the grass, the empty container at her side.

Ben was sitting next to her, still working on his cookies and cream bowl, wanting to make it count since he didn't indulge too often, wanting to stay in playing shape.

"I just love how they put the spoon with the leftover Nutella on it in the cup." Her lips curved, though her eyes were shut. That was okay. He was keeping track of the boys. Not that he needed to, considering that once Brit had caught wind of ice cream—shamelessly eavesdropping on his conversation with Josh—she'd hijacked his outing with Jordyn and the boys.

He didn't mind. Not *too* much, anyway.

The boys were having a blast, running around with the other kiddos. Stefan and Blane keeping them close and looked after... and busy.

It had to be said.

Busy.

No one was in any particular hurry to head home, even though it was late, and the kids should probably be in bed. Because these Dairy nights didn't happen often. Because family and friend time was hard to come by and pretty limited during the season.

So, they were eating ice cream on a Cheat Day (well, calling in that Cheat Day a couple of hours early, since technically it didn't begin until midnight).

So, they were eating ice cream on a cool winter evening.

So, they were letting the kids stay up late and be sugar high and shooting the shit...

And he was next to the woman he'd decided was his.

Jordyn sighed, rolling over on the blanket he'd spread out on the grass. He always kept one in his trunk, just for this reason.

Though, truthfully, it was probably the only time he'd used it for an almost midnight picnic of ice cream with his teammates around while he was sitting beside a woman he was really beginning to care about.

Not beginning.

Cared.

Either way, he had a smile on his lips as he watched her.

"It's like a little treat," she said. "You know?"

He had no idea what the fuck she was talking about.

He'd been watching the way the moonlight had turned her skin almost silver, entranced by the curve of her lips, now tipped up into a smile. He'd been focused on the curves of her body—on that ass he wanted to smack as he pumped into her, hips that were made to grab on to, breasts that made a man lose his focus.

Kind of like right then.

"No, sweetpea."

"Were you even listening?" Generally, that was a dangerous question when a woman asked it of him.

But Jordyn was relaxed, those lips still tipped up, her head still propped up on one hand.

Her eyes were open now and filled with curiosity as she stared at him.

"No," he admitted.

Laughter in those eyes, bubbling off those lips that drove him to insanity. "At least he's honest?" she teased. "So tell me, hockey hot shot, what were you thinking about if you weren't listening to me prattle on about ice cream?"

He didn't know what devil inside him had him saying it.

He just knew that he *was* saying it.

"Your breasts."

Laughter disappeared. Those lips parted.

But he kept going anyway.

"I swear to fuck, I'd pay a king's ransom to see them." His voice was raspy, almost guttural. "More to touch them, to taste them, to suck on them."

SEVENTEEN

JORDYN

I *swear to fuck, I'd pay a king's ransom to see them. More to touch them, to taste them, to suck on them.*

Ho-*ly*. He-*ll*.

Her mouth dropped open. She knew it did.

But she couldn't keep it in place.

Not when his hazel eyes sparked gold, reflections from the strings of lights woven through the trees overhead intertwined with...

Heat.

And that...

Well, after everything went down with Daniel...it felt great.

He was attracted to her. He liked her boobs.

"An-anything else?"

One brow lifted.

"Anything else you like about me?"

Ben reached forward, fingers trailing along the triangle she'd created with her arm and head, her palm on the side of her face, holding it up. Rough fingertips brushed along the sensitive skin on the inside of her arm, something that shouldn't have made her shiver considering she was wearing a hoodie, but something that still did.

She was attracted to this man.

And that was terrifying.

And that was...exhilarating.

And that was what made her bold enough to ask that question, to wait for the answer—though, she couldn't lie. Some part of her expected it to cut.

Because Daniel—his words, his actions, his treatment of her —had cut.

Deeply.

"Besides that kind heart and whip-smart brain?" he asked gently, smoothing his knuckles over her cheek in that gentle way of his, as though somehow seeing the dings in her confidence, the holes in her heart and wanting to buff them out, to fill them in.

He wouldn't hurt her.

This man...

He *wouldn't.*

She felt that in her belly, in her heart, in every neuron in her brain. He was safe. *He* was kind. He—

"Yeah," she whispered and there was more than a bit of wicked in those gorgeous eyes when she added, "I mean something more than my heart and mind."

A thumb tracing over her bottom lip. "Your breasts are fucking perfect," he rumbled, leaning closer, the heat of his breath on her skin. "But I dream about your hips, sweetpea."

"My h-hips?" she stammered out. His eyes were...a maelstrom that threatened to sweep her under.

As though he'd just pulled back the curtain and...

All his desire for her was on full, intense display.

And for a woman who'd spent the last six months feeling unattractive, unwanted, the years before that uncomfortable in her body following two pregnancies that had come close together, with a husband who hadn't appreciated the curves, who'd preferred *"willowy"* body types and hadn't been shy in telling her that...

To be *wanted*...

To feel attractive...

To have a man looking at her like she was fucking Aphrodite striding naked out of the waves...

She inhaled sharply.

It meant a lot, probably more than it should have, but...

It also had her feeling like herself. Her *old* self. The self she'd thought long dead and buried. But now she was realizing that it was very much alive and it liked the way that Ben's words made her feel. *Really* liked the confidence it sparked inside her.

She wouldn't let anyone make her feel that quiet, dead way again.

She'd grab on to freedom and life and living and—

Her lips tipped up.

And she'd get the fuck out of her own head and *live*.

Starting with the man in front of her.

His thumb traced over her mouth again, and it wasn't the light brush from before, but a stronger press, the top dipping into the heated dampness of her mouth.

Reminding her of all the other *damp* things she would like him to dip into.

"My hips?" she asked again, surer this time.

He pulled back, sprawled onto the blanket next to her, and did her breath catch with all the strength of his body so near hers?

Hell yes, it did.

"Yeah," he said, a rough agreement as he tucked his hands behind his head. "Your hips."

Not a lot of words.

But enough to tell her that he'd been thinking plenty about her hips.

"What else?" she pressed, feeling deliciously wicked.

Wicked.

Her.

She smiled and it was wide and probably goofy as hell. But *she* was feeling wicked...at least until he rolled to face her, mirroring her position, propping his head up with his hand. *Then* she wasn't feeling anything, or maybe she was feeling too much—need and desire coiling in her belly, heat and a throbbing ache between her thighs, wicked and confident, unsure and unsteady...

Those knuckles brushed her cheek, touched the curve of her smile, and she opened her eyes, saw that he'd rolled toward her, brought their bodies close together.

Close enough to touch if she shifted just the tiniest bit.

Close enough that his scent was in her nose,

Close enough that—

"What else?" he repeated softly.

The same question, but she heard it anyway.

He was giving her a choice.

To stop this and lean in to the unsure and unsteady.

Or to grasp on to the freedom and dive right into that pool of wicked and confident.

The weight of that choice sat on her chest, as heavy as an elephant.

Then...

She felt the whisper of the cool night air on her skin, the cushion of the grass beneath her body. The softness of the blanket beneath her palm. She looked into hazel eyes and *saw.*

What her future could be.

How her future could be.

And she didn't ask him to tell her what else he liked about her.

She didn't need to.

Instead, she shimmied closer, until their bodies were pressed together front to front.

And then...

She kissed him.

For a second, she didn't feel anything, just the press of flesh to flesh. Then, as though her body had seemingly short-circuited, everything suddenly came online. A flash of sensation. His lips on hers, his hand dropping to her waist, pulling her even closer to the heat of him.

He licked at the seam of her mouth, and she let him in.

Instantaneously.

Like her body knew that this man would bring only good things, would make her feel only good things.

And if this kiss was any indication...her body wasn't wrong.

His fingers gripped one of the hips he'd been talking about, bringing her somehow closer, until she felt every taut muscle, every hard inch of him. It made her want, made her desperate to touch. But Daniel hadn't liked her *distracting* him while they had sex, so she didn't immediately give in to that desire.

Not until the thought slid through her mind.

Not until she processed precisely how fucked up that was.

"What?" Ben whispered, pulling back slightly—or well, just pulling back his head.

Enough to stare into her eyes.

"What is it, sweetpea?" He brushed back her hair. "Too much?"

"No," she whispered. "I just...I haven't done this in a long time."

"That's not it." Not pressing. Just...giving her the space to tell him if she wanted.

Their bodies were still plastered together. She could feel him, still like granite, against her belly. Anyone could come around the trees and spot them. They weren't hiding, and the Gold were gossip-hungry.

But he'd felt the change in her.

And he cared more about what was going on with her than any of the rest of it—becoming gossip, continuing the kiss, demanding that she tell him everything.

That unlocked something in her.

Let the words flow free.

"Daniel didn't like me to touch him when we—" She broke

off, pulled back further, so there was space between their bodies, space for her to think. But it was impossible to. She felt like an idiot, and she fought through embarrassment, through the tears in her eyes.

"Baby?" he asked when she didn't finish.

"He didn't like me to touch him," she whispered. "Not when we had sex."

Because it had been just sex with Daniel.

It hadn't meant anything.

Anger flared in Ben's eyes, but his words were mild. "He was an idiot."

Her lips twitched. "Yeah, I'm starting to realize that."

"And just saying"—his mouth tipped up—"you can touch me anytime—and any*where*—you want."

That...shouldn't have meant as much as it did.

But she couldn't lie. Those words, that assurance, settled deep, warmed her through and through, gave her the confidence to reach forward with her free hand and to press it to his chest.

His heart thudded beneath her palm, beneath his rib cage.

And then, she found that she could shift closer, could press her mouth to his.

Eighteen

"Ah, Benny boy. You know you love me."

It was after two in the morning.

Prior to standing in his open front door, he'd been getting ready to hop into bed, and it had been after a long, hot shower where he'd stroked himself to completion, thinking about that kiss, thinking about *all* the kisses—their first and the later ones they'd snuck on the cool grass under the moonlight. They'd kissed until her boys had shouted her name, had come tearing back over to them, knocking her back onto the blanket, both of them having sat up hastily at the sounds of the boys' voices.

Somehow, they hadn't been seen.

But there hadn't been time for more kissing, more time spent against that lush body of hers that drove him crazy. Not when Jordyn had needed to get the boys home and into bed, weekend or not, it was well past any semblance of bedtime.

So, he'd walked them to her car.

Then, though he'd racked his brain as hard as he could, he hadn't had any further excuse to stay with them.

He'd had to let them go.

Even if it felt like a piece of his heart had gone with them.

Ridiculous.

Maybe only slightly less ridiculous than him having relived that kiss, over and over again.

Until that long, hot shower. Until he'd come, his orgasm leaving his knees weak and thighs shakier than after a playoff game that had gone into double overtime.

He'd managed to drag himself out of the water, to dry off and then hitch a towel around his waist when his doorbell had rung, and he'd known instantly who was standing on his porch.

Middle of the night?

There was only one possibility as to who it was.

He'd tugged on his jeans, pulled on a shirt, shoved his feet into shoes.

He'd hardened his heart, locked down his anger, refused to allow himself to feel anything.

Because he couldn't allow Maddy any opening.

Because she wouldn't go quietly into the good night.

She'd kick. She'd scream. She'd punch and bite and scratch.

That was the Maddy who was at the door, the Maddy who'd come to his place at two in the morning. Only *she* would act like that, wouldn't give one fuck about hurting him in a multitude of ways. That Maddy was a completely different Maddy from the Maddy he loved, from the sister he adored and would do anything for. Totally different from the Maddy who was sober, who'd stopped drinking and wouldn't dream of hurting a fly, let alone making a scene at two in the morning.

But when she stopped being sober, when she began drinking again...that was when *this*—he mentally waved a hand in front of him—happened.

His sister stood in front of him, slurring her words, wavering on her feet as she stood on his porch in the middle of the night.

And unfortunately, she'd picked tonight.

When he'd wanted to think only of Jordyn and her boys, of the way Jordyn's kisses had felt, how much he fucking loved her body. He wanted to think of their ice cream-coated smiles and their protests as Jordyn had ushered them to the car, neither of them wanting to leave the party, even though those smiles were punctuated with yawns. He wanted to think about the warm way she'd stared into his eyes, how her fingers had found his and squeezed lightly before she'd gotten into her car and driven away.

He wanted to think about *that* kiss.

Her tongue.

Her breasts.

Her—

His sister, seemingly having lost patience with him, tried to slither by him and into his house.

"Sit down," he ordered, snagging her shoulder, and forcing her to her ass on the top step, legs sprawling down the other two, not about to let her inside.

He'd made that mistake before and wouldn't make that again.

"Bennie," she slurred, having a hard time staying upright, unable to remain stable even with half of her body on the ground.

"Sit," he said again, reaching into his pocket and extracting his cell, glad he'd stopped and picked up his keys and phone on the way to answer the peals of the doorbell.

That was plural.

Because drunk Maddy was impatient.

And her temper was cobra-like, ready to lash out at the slightest wrong move.

His crime?

They were many. But tonight, there were three: not letting her inside, calling the rehab facility Josh had pulled all sorts of strings to help Ben get her into, and...

Packing her into his car and bringing her back.

When she was sober...she wanted to get better.

When she was drunk...

"It's your fault," she accused, the words not entirely clear, but he'd heard them before. "It's your fault that he left, and it's *your* fault that h-he—"

"It's my fault he touched you," he finished for her, well familiar with the accusation.

Well familiar with the guilt.

If he'd stayed instead of going off to college, crawling his way through the ranks until he made it to the Gold, things might have been different.

His mom might not have gotten involved with Bill.

Maddy wouldn't have been molested.

Maddy wouldn't have numbed herself with alcohol, with drugs, with anything that took the memories away.

"It's my fault you started drinking," he said. "It's my fault you started doing the drugs."

Silence greeted him instead of agreement, instead of more vitriol.

Fine with him.

It made the drive back to the rehab facility shorter.

It made the goodbyes they exchanged—those being none today from her, his usual "goodbye" and "see you soon" from him —easier.

It made the guilt—

No. Nothing made the guilt easier or helped it go away.

Nothing made the fact that *this* Maddy existed any better, and definitely not watching her walk away from him, shoulders slumped, light and warmth completely ripped away from her, *his* sister nowhere to be found.

He couldn't go back.

He couldn't change what had happened.

He *could*, however, do his best for her and his mom now.

But it wouldn't ever be enough.

It wouldn't bring the light and warmth back, wouldn't erase the painful memories, the trauma, make Maddy's need to self-medicate with alcohol go away.

Being here for her now wouldn't change what had happened.

———

He didn't sleep that night.

He didn't dream about kisses or lie in bed thinking about Jordyn and all the ways her body and soul called to his.

He didn't bask in the warmth in her eyes, soak in the comfort that while he hadn't been there for Maddy, he was helping Jordyn, helping keep the light in her eyes, in the boys' eyes.

He sat on his deck for long hours, trying to beat back the memories.

Failing.

So, then he'd gone inside to his office and sat at his desk.

He'd booted up his laptop.

And he'd begun searching.

He knew that Jordyn was struggling to find a job that would pay enough and give her the flexibility to be there for her boys— he'd heard her talking to Josh about it.

Ben could search through job websites, could spend hours weeding through useless job descriptions and shitty ass starting pay.

He wasn't going to sleep.

He might as well make something productive out of it.

Plus, after hours of searching, hours of staring at his laptop's screen, he'd accumulated enough job listings that didn't immediately make him want to chuck his computer through the window.

He sent those over to Josh, since he didn't have Jordyn's email.

Then he went upstairs and packed for the road trip.

The plus of not sleeping and instead spending hours searching?

He was early for the bus.

Nineteen

"And that's the starting salary."

She blinked.

She knew she did.

She tried to hold it back, to pretend that she wasn't reeling inside, because that number was a fuck of a lot different than what she'd seen online, so while her mouth didn't fall open, she couldn't hold back that wide-eyed blink.

Because *what the fuck?*

He was looking at her, his expression one of such pride, like she owed him all the fucking gold stars in the world, that she wanted to reach across the big, fancy, masculine desk he was sprawled behind and throttle it off his face.

But he was looking at her, waiting for her to reply.

She supposed telling him he could fuck right off with that offer wasn't the right course of action.

After all, that shitty ass offer might be the best she could find.

"That's quite a large difference from what was listed on the job description and what you're telling me today."

A shrug. "There's always a range." He held up her resumé.

"Your last office experience was..." His eyes drifted over the paper, probably seeing right through the bullshit she'd been attempting to spin on that page.

So, she didn't bother to pretend.

She just told him the truth.

"Ten years," she said, biting back a sigh.

"So you might be a little out of practice with how this"—he gestured between them—"all works."

The *little lady* vibes were *all* over that statement.

Hell, they were all over this entire building, stuffed full in this office, clogging the air, dripping from the ceiling, sitting heavy on her lungs, making her skin crawl, filling her belly with bile.

She couldn't work here.

She *couldn't.*

Her nostrils flared on an inhale. She held it through her heavy, burning lungs, held it long enough for her to get her temper in check.

Then she stood up, not giving a fuck that he was still talking about the office, or maybe he was just talking about himself now.

Either way, it didn't matter.

She was done here.

Bending, she snagged her purse then straightened again. Then *bent* again, though this time it was to snatch her resumé—and the paper application they'd had her fill out in the lobby area (even though she'd filled out one online...and that right there should have told her to cut her losses immediately)—off his desk.

He sputtered.

Jordyn didn't bother to say another word, just spun on her heel and walked out of the office.

And *God,* it felt fucking great.

So much so that she took the boys to the Dairy after school and they gorged themselves on giant sundaes, cups full to the brim with ice cream and toppings, including an entire cone that the boys used as a receptacle to shovel the treat into their mouths even faster.

Sundaes masquerading as ice cream cones.

Best. Ever.

And she felt that way all the way home, felt it as she parked in the garage, moved into the house, the boys tearing off to their room as she putzed around the kitchen, sorting dinner—though that would be in a couple of hours, since her belly was full of ice cream.

The boys would probably be hungry in fifteen minutes, the tiny little balls of ravenous beasts they were.

Luckily, they had homework to do.

Something she called down the hall and reminded them of... and received begrudging agreements to begin in return.

They'd eat in front of the TV, she thought.

She'd be the super fun mom—ice cream for a snack, dinner late because they'd eaten too much junk food and in front of the TV without anything pesky like conversation. Though, forcing them to do their homework probably took her out of the running for that particular honor, she thought, finding Sammy a pencil when he needed it for his math worksheet.

He was determined to learn how to use his right hand to complete it, even though he was a lefty.

So the neatness of his work might leave much to be desired.

But she was proud of him for trying.

She made a mental note to check with him later and spent a few minutes working on the bedroom lock—she didn't have Jess's or the boys' knack for fixing it and instead of getting it unstuck, she managed to make it not lock at all, even though it still made the *clicky* lock sound and everything. Another doorknob was on her list of things to pick up, apparently. But as long as she wasn't going to end up locked in, she didn't really mind. She didn't have any privacy when it came to the boys anyway.

Failure at DIY firmly put behind her, she poked her head in on each of the boys, checking to make sure Sammy's work was legible and Marcus was hard at work.

His assignment was reading, which suited him fine and meant

that he'd be set for a little while, so she decided to spend some time in the guest bedroom—aka her office thanks to the desk in the corner and the laptop she'd stashed on top—and search through some more job listings.

She'd reached the last of her interviews, and the one job she'd thought was the best fit, was the most excited about, she hadn't gotten.

That email had been waiting for her after she'd dropped the boys that morning.

She needed a job.

She couldn't keep letting Josh take care of her and the boys and her reserves were running pathetically low, and Daniel had refused to send more.

So she'd need money for a lawyer.

She didn't want anything to do with Daniel, didn't want him around her boys if she could help it (though she understood that might not be a reality, at least Josh's lawyer had done the proper paperwork for her to make sure that happened legally and Daniel had signed off on it...another thing she owed her brother for).

But he needed to take care of Sammy and Marcus, financially at the very least.

See?

She was growing her spine back.

Unfortunately, that wasn't going to pay the growing pile of bills on her desk.

Sigh.

She started to pull up the job listing site, wanting to check and see if something had been posted since she'd checked...a full twelve hours before.

But she couldn't make herself hit enter to load the site.

Instead, she clicked over to her email.

Kill time by wading through a plethora of spam messages? Her inbox was always clogged with it. That task alone would keep her busy for a solid ten minutes.

Would distract her from the weight of all the things she needed to do for at least half that time.

Lips tipping up at her thoughts, she began the onerous task of email slogging.

Which was marginally better than job site slogging.

Click. Click. Click.

Deleting all the newsletters she was signed up for because she'd spent more of her time shopping online than in person—none of which she actually opened, and also none of which she actually unsubscribed from either...because she was saving them for the odd chance that she might need a twenty-percent-off from that retailer at some point in the future.

Who knew when she might need it?

Also, who wanted to open all of them, scroll down, locate and then click that little unsubscribe button at the bottom of the email?

No one.

Least of all her.

So she did her clicky-clicking and her deleting without opening and managed to clear most of her inbox.

Amongst the slop were a few important emails—reminders from the school and the boys' teachers, a note from Marcus's soccer coach (Sammy was skipping this season because of his arm) about practice changing time and location, and something from her brother.

With the subject line *Check This Out!!!*

Yup.

Three exclamation points.

Which made the message sound like something that definitely could have come from her grandma, one of those forwarded chain emails that somehow still managed to exist even though everyone knew they were total crap.

But since it was from Josh (she confirmed the address because she was a cynical woman nowadays) and sent early the previous morning (when he'd been on the bus on his way to the airport for the Gold's road trip), she knew that it wasn't some sort of nefarious phishing scheme to get all her details.

It *was* a forwarded message, though.

Forwarded from...

Ben.

Her heart leaped in her chest, bouncing off her rib cage like a rubber ball.

One that had been launched against a wall all over again when she actually took in the contents that Ben had sent to Josh, to send to her.

Thought these might be helpful for Jordyn in her search.

-B

And beneath that was a list of jobs looking for applications.

She clicked on a couple, heart still thudding, her breath coming in short bursts as she read the descriptions, as she took in the details.

Jobs she'd never come across.

Descriptions that *fit* her in a way that she hadn't realized before.

Jobs that fit her life better than anything she'd found.

Ben had done that.

She'd kissed him, let him hold her close, because she liked him, because he was great with the boys and they liked him almost as much as they liked their Uncle Josh.

But...*this?*

This made her fall in love with him, just a little bit.

Which was why she did what she did next.

TWENTY

Ben

The hit took his breath away, but he didn't mind.

He needed the crush against his body, the discomfort, the slice of pain that shot through his arm as he was slammed into the boards.

He could do with the hit not having come from Lake Jordan, the captain of the Sierra.

Lake was talented, pretty, and a fucking terror to play against.

He was *everywhere* and he was strong and he never gave up.

Tenacious fucker.

But Ben was tenacious himself, and he was in a shit mood, and he was feeling really fucking mean, so he shoved Lake off, taking no little amount of satisfaction in the fact that he fell back and landed on his ass.

Ha.

Fucker.

He kicked the puck from where he'd been protecting it between his feet up to his stick, immediately taking off for the net, driving through the defenseman who came up to challenge him.

Normally, he would have looked for a pass.

Normally, he wouldn't have been like a fucking bull charging for a matador's muleta, the red of the goalposts practically calling to him like that red fabric did a bull.

But he wasn't feeling very normal.

Hadn't been since he'd dropped his sister back off at rehab.

Or maybe he was feeling *back* to normal, that cold sitting heavy on his chest, sinking into his stomach.

The happiness he'd found with the team was what was abnormal.

The happiness he'd found with Jordyn—

A slash to his stick snapped him to rigid focus.

He shoved Maddy roughly from his mind. He shoved Jordyn, albeit more gently, because he needed her out, but he didn't ever want to hurt her.

He shoved the night at the Dairy, the way Sammy had held tight to him when he'd been hurt.

He shoved all that made him feel warm away.

Deep, deep away.

Hockey was safe.

Hockey was it.

Hockey was all he could have, could be trusted to have.

Better he remembered that now than at some point in the future.

Better—

Another slash, a body crashing into his, slowing his progress to the net, he sucked in a breath, pushed off, gained a few more feet, and this time he looked up, saw Will was open at the back door.

He did what he did best—stopped thinking about what wasn't on the ice—focused his mind on the game, on his teammates, on that fucking goal he was getting closer to, but still wasn't clear to.

But Will had a clear shot.

Will was open.

He turned off everything that wasn't hockey and passed the puck over to Will.

Who didn't miss a beat, just slammed it home.

The crowd booed. Lake Jordan shoved him hard as he skated by Ben and moved to his bench. Fucker. But Ben understood the other man's frustration.

His own was roiling beneath his skin.

And it had absolutely nothing to do with hockey.

———

Luckily, he was one of the quieter guys in the locker room, so his broody silence didn't immediately trigger anyone's concern.

But it would become noticeable at some point.

They were nosy fuckers, a pushy, loud, close family, and sooner or later they would recognize that his head was fucked up again.

Which meant he needed to get his shit together.

Easy said.

Hard to do.

He inhaled, held it for long enough to make his lungs burn, and then released it slowly.

"You were on fucking fire, man," Rome said from next to him. He, Will, Rome, and Lucas, had joined the team around the same time. Along with Axel, a newer addition who'd recently been pulled up permanently from the team's minor league affiliate, the Rush, rounded out the rookie corner of the locker room.

It made it easier to slide under the radar—minus the fact that Brit seemed to have an instinctual affinity for ferreting out anyone who was at risk of drowning.

So far...

Axel had been subject to a few Brit talks.

Today?

It was Will.

"Thanks," he told Rome, fist-bumping his teammate, but deliberately keeping his focus on undressing.

Because Brit's laser gaze had gone to Will.

She was sitting next to him, having squeezed her way in between him and Lucas, who was on Ben's left.

A hockey player barrier between him and Brit, her focus on Will.

But he still needed to be careful to not draw attention.

All of that being said, he was still a nosy motherfucker.

He had that hockey player barrier between him and Brit—in the form of Lucas—but he was listening intently (and not to Rome).

He was listening to the snippets of what Will was saying to Brit.

Because Will had been off lately.

And he wanted to know why.

Look at him being a fucking hypocrite.

That fact didn't stop him from hearing Will say, "It's nothing, Brit. I'm fine."

Liar.

He didn't need to call him on that—Brit had him covered. "Bullshit," she said. "I can see it on your face, Will. What's going on?"

Will was quiet for a long moment. "Look," he finally said. "I'm not ready to talk about it."

Brit didn't miss a beat. "You should—"

"I'm *not* ready to talk about it."

"Will—"

He spun to face Brit—and subsequently caught Ben and Lucas listening in as well. His eyes flashed, but he looked at each of them. "Yes, it's about a woman." He shook his head. "Yes, it's fucking with my head." His eyes narrowed. "No, I don't want to talk about it, or need any help with it, or want you fuckers poking your noses in it." A breath. "No offense meant."

The half of Brit's mouth that Ben could see tipped up. "None taken."

She fell silent after that.

But only for a couple of heartbeats.

Then she said, a bit of wicked curling into the edges of her voice. "Are you sure?"

Will *thunked* his head against the wall.

"Just saying"—she was laughing now, and for what it was worth, so was Will—"we're really good at fixing women problems."

Will turned to look at her, but his gaze seemed to catch on Ben's, seemed to see what was happening in Ben's own head, and he said, "I know."

———

Ice still in his veins after he'd made it into his hotel in Colorado hours later, he flopped onto the mattress and pulled out his phone.

He needed the banality of cake-decorating YouTube videos.

His secret pleasure.

But it wasn't doing much for him tonight.

Absentmindedly, he clicked over to his email.

And...

His heart stopped.

The cold was washed away.

Jordyn had sent him an email.

It was silly how quickly his heart started back up, how quickly it was pounding against his rib cage, how quickly it took his breath away.

Then he sucked in a breath, released it slowly, and tapped the message, eyes flying across the words, moving so fast that he had to stop and go to the beginning and reread the entire thing again just to process it.

He was smiling. Huge.

And the message was just a thank you for the job listings.

Nothing poetic or particularly romantic.

Just Jordyn sending him a quick note.

Except...she hadn't just replied to the email Josh had forwarded to her, hadn't told her brother to thank him. She'd realized he'd sent the listings, had taken the extra step to locate his email and message him directly.

That...

Was nothing.

But it was also kind of *something*.

He relaxed against the pillows, holding his phone to his chest like a kid cuddling a stuffed toy.

Then he realized he was still smiling.

Huge.

Because of Jordyn.

Because she'd reached out to him. She'd made the effort for *him*.

He hadn't had that.

Not from his family. Not from anyone but his teammates and their people.

His dad had left when he was eight.

His mom relied on him to make all the effort. Even now, even with her supposedly having turned over a new leaf, wanting a different relationship with him, nothing had changed. Not even when she had come to fill his fridge—that supposed act of kindness was because she'd wanted him to go to the rehab. She hadn't wanted to come see him.

Not really.

But someone he really cared about? Someone he might be in love with, just a little bit (maybe more) doing something for him?

That meant a lot.

That had the cold melting away, the urge to lock up and keep everyone at a distance gone like so much smoke. He didn't want Jordyn to stay away. He wanted her close. He wanted to keep knowing the woman who'd already made a place for herself in his heart.

If he locked down, closed up, she would—

Well, how could he know her more if he kept her out?

He couldn't.

His biological family was fucked up. But his Gold one wasn't.

What Jordyn had made free of her douchebag of an ex wasn't.

What they might create together wouldn't be.

He knew that with every fiber of his being.

And that had his fingers moving on his phone typing out a message that was probably stupid as fuck, but one that kept the smile on his face.

One that would hopefully bring the same smile to Jordyn's.

Twenty-One

From: Ben Roberts <ben.roberts@gold.com>
To: Jordyn Webb <jordyn@webb.com>
Subject: re: Thank you
Jor,
You can thank me in Dairy ice cream (and peanut-butter-flavored kisses) next Cheat Day.
-B

From: Jordyn Webb <jordyn@webb.com>
To: Ben Roberts <ben.roberts@gold.com>
Subject: re: Thank you
Ben,
You're on. But I'm not sure that cookies and cream goes with peanut butter.
-J

P.S. Sammy wanted me to send you a picture of his latest Lego creation (I attached it below).

From: Ben Roberts <ben.roberts@gold.com>
To: Jordyn Webb <jordyn@webb.com>
Subject: re: Thank you
Jor,
You know it does.
-B
P.S. Tell Sammy he's a rockstar master builder. That's impressive, especially with one arm still in a cast.

From: Jordyn Webb <jordyn@webb.com>
To: Ben Roberts <ben.roberts@gold.com>
Subject: re: Thank you
Ben,
I agree. I *do* know that cookies and cream and peanut butter go well together. So much so that my cheeks are hot and I'm huffing and puffing as I'm walking up this giant ass hill to pick up the kids from school (and trying to pretend that I'm not so out of shape that a five-minute walk is making me out of breath) as I remember.
Or maybe it's because I'm remembering the way you kissed me.
-J
P.S. Sammy said that was the BEST COMPLIMENT EVER! (Or yelled it, rather).

From: Ben Roberts <ben.roberts@gold.com>
To: Jordyn Webb <jordyn@webb.com>

Subject: re: Thank you

Jor,

I'm taking it as my kisses are what makes you out of breath.

-B

P.S. I want to be Sammy when I grow up. All that enthusiasm and drive in a tiny six-year-old's body? He's going to be unstoppable when he's an adult.

P.P.S. Tell Marcus with all of his reading, he's going to take over the world. Either that, or become the CEO of a billion-dollar company, or—well, he's so smart that the sky's the limit.

From: Jordyn Webb <jordyn@webb.com>
To: Ben Roberts <ben.roberts@gold.com>
Subject: re: Thank you

Ben,

I've got great news today! I had an interview and it went GREAT! Yes, all caps, Sammy-style GREAT! I think it might really work out and we were vibing, and I think I might actually get it. AND it's work from home and my—hopefully—soon-to-be manager has school-aged kids. So she gets it. Which is perfect. And it's all thanks to you. Which means that I owe you my special cinnamon sugar bread. Your next Cheat Day is going to be LIT! (More Sammy energy there for you). Good luck in the game tonight! Only two more until you guys are back at the Gold Mine. I bet you're ready to be back on home ice...and back in your bed (and that's said with a dash of Jordyn-who-likes-your-kisses spirit...even though it's making my cheeks hot again).

-J

P.S. Maybe I shouldn't say this, but...I miss you.

P.P.S. Marcus wanted me to attach the "book" he wrote for school. He wanted you to read it, but I told him that you probably won't have time to read it because you're busy doing things like—you know—playing hockey :)

. . .

From: Ben Roberts <ben.roberts@gold.com>
To: Jordyn Webb <jordyn@webb.com>
Subject: re: Thank you
Jor,
Congrats on the interview, sweetpea. They'd be lucky to have you. Let me know one way or the other as soon as you hear.
Side note, I think all this talk of sundaes and cinnamon sugar bread means that my next Cheat Day is yours. But be forewarned, I promise that I'm going to try to sneak a few kisses. I KNOW (that's with Sammy enthusiasm) that cinnamon and sugar taste best when I'm licking it off your lips.
-B
P.S. Tell Marcus to forget taking over the world. He's going to be a bestselling author, no doubt.
P.P.S. Also, I need to know what happens to Steve. Did he ever get out of the well?

From: Jordyn Webb <jordyn@webb.com>
To: Ben Roberts <ben.roberts@gold.com>
Subject: re: Thank you
Ben,
I GOT THE JOB!!!
-J
P.S. Despite all your talk of stealing kisses...I think *you're* the one who's going to be on the receiving end of my stealthy efforts.
You'd better watch out. You might have the hockey player reflexes, but *I've* got a hockey player for a big brother and he taught me all his tricks.

From: Ben Roberts <ben.roberts@gold.com>
To: Jordyn Webb <jordyn@webb.com>
Subject: re: Thank you
Jor,
I'm so proud of you.
-B
P.S. Thanks for that. I needed good news today.

From: Jordyn Webb <jordyn@webb.com>
To: Ben Roberts <ben.roberts@gold.com>
Subject: re: Thank you
Ben,
Why? What's wrong?
-J

From: Ben Roberts <ben.roberts@gold.com>
To: Jordyn Webb <jordyn@webb.com>
Subject: re: Thank you
Jor,
Family crap. I...sometimes they make it really hard to love them.
My sister and mom, that is.
-B

She frowned at the last message from Ben, worry curling in her belly.

On the one hand, he was opening up to her.

On the other, he sounded like he was hurting.

A lot.

And it wasn't just pain from the present. It was hurt from the past mixing with that of the present. And she knew something of pains tangling together, turning into something heavy that hung from her neck.

She was...coming out of that.

She had a job offer and a way forward on the house. Last night, she'd come out of the office, had seen the boys curled up on the couch, watching crappy YouTube videos on TV while they played a board game.

Junk everywhere.

Shoes and pants (don't ask, Sammy liked to be "comfortable") and wrappers. Board game pieces and crumbs.

And she'd realized they'd made this place home.

She could too.

So, she was going to stop fighting their kindness, going to make sure she found a way to pay for the house, even if that meant busting her ass and scrimping and saving everywhere she could.

Because this was the path forward.

Just deciding that, just giving in a little, not feeling as though she had to fight every bit of help, had to *prove* to the world that she could do it on her own, understanding—finally—in that moment of chaos, of seeing her boys happy and satisfied, even though it *wasn't* perfect, wasn't clean, wasn't watching some perfectly educational program eating whole, healthy food had freed something in her.

She didn't need to keep trying to be perfect.

Daniel had expected her to be, and she'd tried to be, desperate to make him happy.

But...he never would have been happy with her, no matter what she did, no matter how many hoops she'd jumped through.

So perfect?

She got to let that go.

Today, *now*, she got to let some other things go. The first being the urge to run through the house, clearing up everything, scrubbing every surface. The second being...

Something that she could think of later. Something that could wait until after her bath.

The boys had new friends and, conveniently, two of those were brothers.

So Marcus and Sammy were at a sleepover (something, heaven help her, she'd agreed to reciprocate in two weeks).

She had the night to herself.

It was going to be glorious, she thought, running her hands through the stream of water that was bordering on a temperature that was just shy of boiling.

Exactly the way she liked it.

She'd boil herself in the tub like she was a crab, and then she'd curl up with a book and read until the wee hours of the morning.

The mess would still be there.

And if she was working on letting the whole perfectionist thing go, then she could accept that the mess would still be there for her to clean up in the morning.

Smiling to herself, she stripped down and wondered when the guys would be home. Their plane had been delayed due to some bad weather back east, so they should be arriving sometime this evening.

And tomorrow was...Cheat Day.

Her smile widened, thinking of those emails and the soon-to-be stolen kisses. *After* she convinced him to tell her why he was struggling with his mom and sister.

But to move things along, she already had the bread proofing in the fridge. Since it was a brioche recipe, it did best with a slow overnight rise.

Tomorrow, she'd load it up with the butter and cinnamon and sugar that made it delicious.

She'd bake it off, slice herself a hunk while she was still hungry because she was always impatient.

Use it to tempt him into sharing some of that hurt, letting her help him sort through it.

And hopefully after that, she'd get to taste the deliciousness on Ben's lips.

That turned her smile full-on smirk.

They'd emailed like they were living in 1998, like they didn't have each other's cell numbers, like they couldn't have called or texted or FaceTimed.

It was different.

But it was also unbelievably sweet.

She'd never been more excited to check her email, and the short notes, the way he'd responded had made her—

Well, that little bit of her that was falling in love with him had fallen harder.

Somehow that wasn't scary, even though it should be.

She wasn't even officially divorced yet.

Maybe not, but for the first time in a long time, she was looking to the future.

"Good," she whispered to herself, lifting her leg and just about to climb into the tub—

The doorbell rang.

"Okay, that's *not* good," she muttered, straightening and moving to the hook where she kept her robe, shrugging into it, securing the tie and moving down the hall—

Just as the bell rang again.

"All right!" she called. "I'm coming!"

She reached for the knob, turned it, pulled the door open.

And—

TWENTY-TWO

BEN

She was standing in front of him in a bathrobe.

Her skin.

So much of her skin was on display.

Long legs he wanted wrapped around his waist. Delicate collarbones he wanted to taste. Breasts—fuck, her breasts undid him completely.

And he stopped thinking about the travel day from hell.

He stopped thinking about the shit his mom had dropped on him.

He stopped thinking about the tense phone call he'd had to undo it.

He stopped thinking about—

Everything.

Dropping his bag—he'd come straight from the practice facility, had driven directly to Jordyn's place.

Needing to see her and the boys.

Which wrenched him back from grabbing her, ripping that robe off, and stealing all those kisses he'd promised he would take.

"The boys?" he rasped.

She blinked, mouth dropping open. "Wh-what?"

A kick slid his bag far enough that he could nudge her back, could step in behind her, could close and lock the door behind them. "Are the boys here?" he asked, his voice like gravel.

"Are you—"

Sammy and Marcus potentially being there or not, he couldn't resist trailing his fingertip over one collarbone then the other.

A shake of her head, eyes seeming to have glazed over.

He bent, flicked his tongue over the skin drawn tight over her collarbones. Trailed one hand up the back of her thigh, up over her ass, and felt nothing but lush, silken flesh.

Fuck.

She tasted like sweet, soft woman.

But she *felt* like a ripe, tempting woman.

And with one tug he could touch all of her, could *taste* all of her.

But he couldn't strip her naked in the hall if they were about to be ransacked by a six- and eight-year-old.

A nip to her throat, his mind telling him it was to focus her, but he knew it was a lie.

He needed to keep tasting her.

She jumped. Her hand came to the back of his head, fingers weaving through his hair pressing to his scalp.

"Sweetpea?" he asked against her skin. "Sammy and Marcus—"

Her fingers tightened against his scalp. "Are at a sleepover."

It came out in a breathless rush, almost indiscernible, especially with his pulse pounding in his ears.

But then he *did* process it and all he could think was...

Thank fuck.

His knees hit the hardwood floor in the hall and he reached for the tie of her robe, tugging it. The fabric parted like the motherfucking Red Sea and since he was already on his knees, he sent up a prayer to whoever the fuck was in charge, thanking them for the fucking *beauty* that was standing in front of him.

She started to reach for the fabric, catching it as it slid down her arms, grabbing it before it fell off her hands.

A blip of insecurity on her face.

"No," he said, staying her when she would have covered herself. "No, sweetpea. You're beautiful."

Teeth pressing into a bottom lip. Releasing. "I—my stomach is—"

"Your stomach is part of you," he murmured before he leaned forward, pressed a kiss to the soft curve of her belly, to the faint lines that showed she'd carried her two boys. "And so are these. They show that you carried your boys, honey. They show your strength."

Tears glimmering in her eyes. "I'm not sure I see it that way."

"Don't worry." Another kiss to the small curve. "You'll get there."

A spark in her eyes. A glimpse of fire that went straight to his cock. "You think so?"

He *thought* he was going to love this woman so much that she wasn't going to so much as dare to not love every fucking millimeter of herself—from her toes polished pink to her legs he was desperate to get between, to her stomach and breasts and arms and throat and face.

There wasn't one piece of her he didn't adore.

Now it had become his life's mission to get her to see the same thing.

"Yeah, sweetpea," he said. "I do." Then he nudged her back again, only this time at an angle, pressing her to the wall...and using her moment of distraction to pick up one of those gorgeous legs and toss it over his shoulder.

She *did* taste like a soft, sweet woman.

"Ben!" she gasped.

His tongue sliding through slick folds, his hand with a palmful of that ass he fucking *loved*, tugging her against him, kissing her with every bit of focus he could muster. Hard when all the blood in his body was moving south, but easy when her hand dove into his hair again, held him to her, hips beginning to rock when he found the right spot.

"I—*oh*"—her head *thunked* back against the wall, rattling one of the pictures—"*oh,* God. That's—"

She broke off again when he sucked hard on her clit, standing leg trembling so hard that he was worried she was going to fall.

Gripping her other leg, he lifted it at the same time he stood, sliding her back up the wall, using it and his hold to take her weight, shoulders spreading her wide.

"Don't stop," she gasped, fingers clinging to his hair, pulling so hard that his scalp stung.

And he didn't give a fuck.

Because her body was trembling now.

Because her skin was sheeted in sweat.

Because—

A gush of liquid on his tongue, coating the outside of his mouth, and—

She screamed, head dropping back again, coming apart on his lips, his tongue, on *him.* He caught all the pieces, helped her through to the other side.

He knew she was coming back into herself when he slid her down his body, made sure she was steady on her feet, and her lips turned up. "Talk about a stolen kiss."

Laughter snuck out of him, which was a fucking miracle, considering he was wound so tight that he was ready to explode, that he was desperately trying to find some control, some strength to not fuck her right there in the hall.

She had a little table he could bend her over, could slide into her from behind, pressing deep, watching that ass of hers jiggle.

The kitchen and its heavy wood table was right behind her.

The couch, if he was searching for something softer, wasn't far down the hall.

Hell, her bedroom wasn't much beyond that.

A hand on his chest had him jumping, eyes flying open.

He was missing her naked. He needed to focus.

"Those look uncomfortable," she murmured, mouth tipping up, hand sliding down, eyes on his pants—on his dick fighting the confines of the material.

"It's fine, sweetpea."

A pause, her eyes coming to his.

She studied him. Then her mouth curved up. "Good guy."

"Wh-what?" Her fingers had reached the waistband of his pants, were drifting back and forth, fingers dipping beneath just the slightest bit...dipping damned close to the head of his cock. Which was fucking weeping for her.

"You're a good guy."

She stepped closer, pressing her body to his, and he felt every inch of her warm, delicious body against him.

"You're trying to find your control."

Yes. That.

"To not fuck me right here in the hall."

A blaze of heat searing through him.

"But"—her lips on his jaw, breath ghosting along his beard, his skin, making him shiver—"here's the thing..."

"Yeah?" he prompted, voice like sandpaper, mostly because her hand was now trapped between them and her fingers were still dipping...only this time they were dipping beneath his underwear, trailing along the head of his cock.

"I'm a mom."

"Yeah?" Another prompt, his focus—and his control—almost completely splintered.

"I'm a mom," she said again, hand dipping further, wrapping around him, squeezing until he saw stars, "so that means I know my kid-free time is limited."

He stilled.

"And tonight I'm kid-free."

She rose on tiptoe, nipped at his earlobe, and he nearly came right there.

"Let's take advantage of it, yeah?"

Somehow she'd unbuttoned his pants, and she shoved them down, exposed him. The sight of her hand wrapped around him—

Fucking motherfucker.

He clenched his jaw until his teeth threatened to turn to dust. "You sure you're ready for this step, sweetpea?" Rasping words. His mind spinning. Cock aching. *His* thighs trembling now. But he had to make sure, had to take care of her.

She took his hand in her free one, brought it between her thighs, brought it to all that liquid heat. "Why don't you feel for yourself and find out?"

And that was when his control splintered.

His wallet was out of his pants a second later, the condom he kept there torn open, rolled down his shaft. A second after that, Jordyn was bent over that table in the hall.

It was closest.

They could explore the others later.

She arched that ass up, flashing that glistening pussy. Hands on the table, eyes on his as she watched him over her shoulder.

He pushed in.

And—

"Fuck," he hissed.

Tight. Hot. Her wetness gathering at the base of his dick, his pelvis. He wanted to feel it skin on skin. He wanted—

She clenched around him. "Hard," she ordered. "Fast, baby. Please."

Hard and fast was all he had in him.

He pulled out, thrust in.

And again.

And *again.*

Until she was bucking against him. Until he was reaching around, circling her clit.

Until she was coming apart.

He was a second behind her, his orgasm tearing through him, and hell if it didn't make his legs give way.

Luckily, he bundled her against his chest, caught her so she didn't get hurt.

The same couldn't be said about his ass.

But even that couldn't take off the edge of his pleasure, couldn't ruin the moment.

Nothing could.

And she proved it when she smiled up at him, breaths still coming a little fast, expression a little dopey, smile languid, like a cat who'd gotten the cream, palm coming to his cheek.

"*And* you didn't even get to my breasts."

Twenty-Three

Jordyn

He moaned.

Her belly clenched.

"This is really good."

Wet between her thighs.

"Really, *really* good, sweetpea."

His knuckles brushed along her cheek, the arm around her waist tugging her closer.

"Yeah?" she murmured, hand going to his bare chest.

Bare because last night they'd made it to the couch.

Had they Instacarted some condoms and DoorDashed some food?

Yes.

Was that probably the most ridiculous thing she'd done in one evening?

Also, yes.

But so worth it because they'd made it to the couch and then to the bedroom and there they'd stayed.

She was sore.

She had been pleasured within an inch of her life.

And the best part?

She'd touched and held him while they made love (*and* was fucked into oblivion), and aside from her initial blip of insecurity, she had felt like herself.

Not second-guessing every touch and moan and position.

Just being with Ben and—

Those orgasms that sent her into the stratosphere.

Now it was morning and the bread was baked and—

Ben approved apparently.

"Taste," he said.

She opened her mouth when he held up the bread, but instead of giving her a bite like she'd expected, he kissed her.

"Hey," she murmured, when they broke apart, "that was *my* plan."

He cupped her cheek. "Glad we're on the same page." A wicked grin. Another kiss. Then he was steering her toward a chair, pushing her down lightly into it. "Want me to cut you a slice?"

"Not gonna give me another taste?" she teased.

"Later," he said. "I've got to make sure I feed you so you can keep up your strength. So"—he kissed the top of her head—"let me wow you with my toast-making ability while you tell me about the job."

She sat back, smiling wide. "It's amazing, baby. I'm really excited about it. I start next week, but they've been so great already. I swear, it's like I've been part of the team for years already. They even..." She told him about the welcome package they sent and the stipend to set up her home office. She waxed poetic about her soon-to-be manager checking in regularly and the email system of all things.

She prattled, probably for too long, but he didn't get impatient or give her the impression that he wasn't interested or had lost focus.

On the contrary, his attention was wholly on her the entire time she talked.

And...just like that, she fell more in love with him, until it wasn't just pieces of her. It was all of her.

But she needed to know him, too.

So, she finished her toast and bucked up the courage to ask, "What's going on with your mom and sister?"

He'd been reaching for another slice of cinnamon sugar bread—perfectly toasted because he had mad toast skills—but her question had him freezing.

And when he looked up at her, his expression sliced deep.

He wasn't going to tell her anything.

Her immediate reaction was to shut down, to call the question back, but...she was learning. She was starting to think closely about why she felt certain things—like wanting to run from that cool look he shot her, even though there wasn't a sliver of anger or a single sharp word.

But wasn't he doing the same thing?

Shutting down? Running?

And seeing that for what it was, knowing that she had very similar reactions, gave her the strength to...well, *give.*

This was a man who'd made her feel comfortable in bed, who'd worshiped her body and given her confidence in herself. This was a man who played with her kids and made her smile and touched her gently and sweetly.

This was a man who made no qualms about the fact that he liked her.

Her.

Not some woman striving for perfection, even knowing she would never get there.

So she could give now.

God knew he'd already proven that he gave for her.

"Daniel wasn't always like he is now," she whispered.

His expression immediately gentled. "Sweetpea," he murmured, reaching for her hand, lacing their fingers together.

"I—we were together since high school, and I swear he treated me well." She rubbed her forehead with her free hand, thinking of the off-again, on-again relationships, the breakups and getting back together, the *drama*. "No," she added. "No, that's actually not right." A sigh. "I made myself smaller, made myself quieter. So we didn't fight. But he was still...Daniel, and he didn't treat me like he should." She nibbled at her lip then blew out a breath. "I let him do that. But I'm not going to let him do that anymore, not going to let *anyone* do that to me again. Though, thankfully, I have a good example *now* of how a man should treat me."

He went still again.

Warm crept into that cool. "Sweetpea."

She slipped from her seat, rounded the table, and plunked into Ben's lap. "It's true," she murmured.

He pressed his face into her hair, inhaled deeply.

And then he proved that he could give, too.

"My dad left when I was eight, and my mom fell apart. She... well, I had to step in and do a lot at home with my sister and with our house. I was paying bills and working a newspaper route by the time I was nine, babysitting every free moment I wasn't in school." Another inhale. Another slow exhale. "It didn't get any easier as time went on, either. Maddy was getting bigger and needing more things, and my mom...fuck, but she'd checked out."

She wrapped her arms around his shoulders, held on tight. "Oh, honey," she whispered.

His palm skated down her spine and back up. "It...my life was for Maddy. And that was fine. But by the time I got a chance to leave for college, she was fourteen, and I thought she was old enough, so I jumped at that opportunity."

Her heart squeezed.

Because she didn't think that went well.

"I was smothered, you know. I just wanted a couple of years to live for myself." He exhaled again. "It turns out that was the worst time for me to have left."

Jordyn braced.

"My mom got remarried. Literally out of the fucking blue. One moment, she was her normal depressed self, barely going to work, barely making enough to pay for them—and taking every penny I was able to send them—and the next, she'd come home with a husband."

She gasped.

"Yeah," he said. "I hadn't met him. Maddy hadn't either. He was just moving in and—" His voice cracked and she knew, *knew* this was about to get bad.

But she didn't push him.

Just held him and waited.

"He raped her. Maddy. He raped her over and over again."

It took everything in her to not gasp again, to just hold on and be there for him.

"And no one knew until she got pregnant just after she'd turned eighteen. She'd started staying out late with her friends, and my mom was worried about that. But she figured it was just high school stuff, that Maddy was pushing the limits."

"It wasn't though."

"No," he whispered. "All those years it wasn't Maddy acting out, wasn't her just ignoring curfew and staying out late. She was partying, drinking, taking drugs, numbing it away, and she did it for years."

"Oh, honey," she whispered.

"I can't blame her for that. I wish she'd told me, but she blamed me for leaving, still does. Both of them do." He sighed. "I can see it in their eyes every time I'm with them. But eventually she got pregnant and went for an abortion. She didn't tell anyone, went out, got drunk, and there were complications. She nearly died of blood loss."

"Shit." Another whisper.

A nod. "Her friend got her to the hospital, and everything came out. Maddy got help, but it wasn't enough. She's been on and off drugs for the last ten years. I've paid for her to go to rehab more times than I can count, but she...I don't know. Maybe she doesn't want to get better."

"Baby," Jordyn whispered, hugging him tight. "I'm so sorry that was done to her."

"Me too."

"And I'm sorry for you, too. And for your mom." Though, frankly, the last was a bit of a lie. Leaving her eight-year-old to hold them together? That was like expecting Marcus to run the house just because Daniel was a fucking douchebag. And then to blame Ben for what happened to his sister?

Honestly, she wanted to throw down with the woman.

"My mom." He sighed, leaning back enough to see her face, probably to identify that train of thought. "I know that I should hate her."

"Hate is a hard feeling to hold on to."

It was why she'd spent so long with Daniel, she supposed—the love and hate and like all mixed together, all tangled up.

"I just...she's weak." He smoothed a hand over her hair. "And I love her."

"So you just...accept her for what she can give you," she murmured. "But you also need to protect yourself. Limit contact if you need, don't let guilt yank you back in."

That hand drifting forward, cupping her jaw. "How'd you get so smart?"

She smiled gently at him. "By being stupid for a really long time."

Twenty-Four

By the time he got home, much later that evening, having gone with Jordyn to pick up the boys from their sleep-over, after which they'd all gone out to a late lunch together, he was exhausted.

Because the late lunch had been followed by an afternoon of playing Legos with the boys and then a late dinner—well, breakfast for dinner, but since it was French toast with cinnamon sugar bread and crispy bacon. And then since it was Cheat Day and they'd hit the Dairy for sundaes afterward, Ben wasn't mad at that exhaustion.

Ice cream.

Peanut butter mixing with cookies and cream.

He was mad—no...it was part physical exhaustion (they'd been up late the night before...exerting themselves and then Marcus and Sammy seemed to have unending energy, even despite the bulky cast on Sammy's arm). The rest of it, of course, was emotional fatigue.

He didn't talk about that shit, hadn't with anyone.

And it was something, with the exception of his mom and Maddy, that no one knew.

Even Josh didn't have the whole story.

Yeah, he knew Ben's sister needed rehab, that Ben needed help getting her to go.

But that was it.

He didn't know about the rest of it.

Sighing, Ben moved through his house, looking at the calendar, making a mental checklist of things that needed to get done, game days, travel days.

It would be busy.

It always was this time of year.

But Marcus had asked him to come to his soccer game that Saturday.

Ben was going to make that happen, even if he had to miss out on a bit of sleep. Because, separate from what he felt for Jordyn, he was falling for those kids too.

Sammy's smile that was so much like Jordyn's it was a sucker punch to the gut every time he saw it.

Marcus's enthusiasm in describing his favorite books, in telling Ben what had happened to Steve in that mine and what was going to happen in the rest of the story he was writing.

He didn't understand what would drive a man to leave those boys.

They were wonderful.

Then again, Daniel had cheated on Jordyn and let her go, so he clearly had no problem letting the best things in life go.

Ben wasn't going to make the same mistake.

So he was going to sacrifice a couple of hours of sleep and get up bright and early after the game on Friday so that he could make Marcus's soccer match.

Then it was late and he was heading to bed.

He slid under the covers, pulled out his cell, clicked into his email, as he'd been doing every night before he went to sleep ever since Jordyn had sent that first message.

Except the previous night, of course.

But as his fingers began to move on the screen, typing out an email, he paused.

Then he clicked on her contact.

Text?

No. He wanted to hear her voice.

Which probably revealed too much, but he supposed Jordyn already knew that he was in deep...and he really wanted to talk to her one more time before he went to sleep.

So he ignored the voice telling him to pull back—because, frankly, it had been telling him that from the beginning and he'd been ignoring it from the beginning and—

He called her.

She picked up on the fourth ring, slightly breathless. "'Ello?"

"Sweetpea."

A moment of quiet and then her voice went soft. "Hey, baby."

Fuck, he loved that.

Fuck, he loved her.

"You getting ready for bed?"

"Trying to," she said and then laughed. "Unfortunately, these demon children have decided that post-sleepover, brekkie for dinner, sundaes, and spending time with their second-favorite hockey player means they don't need pesky things like sleep."

"Second favorite?"

"Uncle Josh decided that he's going to take them to the beach tomorrow."

"Man," he said, laughing, "I guess I've got to up my game."

"Do..."

He waited, pulse picking up.

"D-did you want to come with us?"

"Yes."

No hesitation.

Not with Jordyn.

Not ever.

"Okay," she whispered. "I—we're leaving the house around nine."

"I'll be there."

"Okay," she whispered.

"Okay," he whispered back.

He held the phone to his ear, listening to her breathing, waiting to see if she'd say anything else. She didn't disappoint.

"Josh will be there."

He grinned. "I know, sweetpea."

"Well, you know, he can be a little—" He could almost picture her tilting her head from side to side.

"Protective?" he finished for her.

"He's my older brother," she said softly. "He's always been there for me and…"

The rest of her words were a buzz in his head because he knew she hadn't meant to slice, had just been speaking the truth.

About Josh.

Because Ben…he hadn't always been there.

"*Ben!*"

He blinked. "Yeah, sweetpea."

"You need to stop thinking that." Her tone was firmer than he'd ever heard it.

"I'm fine, honey," he said. "Just tired."

"Bullshit."

He blinked again.

"You're thinking about your own sister." Now she gentled. "I'm sorry, baby. I didn't mean to bring it up, or to make it seem like you weren't there for her."

He hadn't been.

There was no denying it.

"You're allowed to live your life, honey. You're allowed to live it for yourself. Your mom should have—"

There was no denying that either.

But he couldn't talk about this again.

Not today.

Not so soon.

"So how do I go from the boys' second-favorite to first-favorite hockey player?"

Silence.

A sigh rattling through the speakers.

Then, "I'm going to give you that subject change. But just for today."

Firm, firm words.

He remembered the woman he'd met weeks ago, the woman crying those heart-wrenching sobs, the woman with dark shadows beneath her eyes and bruises on her soul.

He'd been called to help her, to protect her.

But he was realizing that she was far stronger than he'd ever given her credit for.

"You're a badass, you know that, right?"

Surprised laughter. "I mean, I *have* an ass. But I don't feel like it's particularly bad."

"I mean it, sweetpea. You're..." He blew out a breath. "I'm in awe of your strength."

More quiet, but this time it wasn't of the ticked-off variety.

"Back at you, hotshot." A beat. "And the way to get to the top of that list is to come through on the Lego Falcon. Even Joshie can't compete with that."

His smile flashed again. "Done."

She giggled then yawned and he heard her settling into bed, the rustle of the sheets and comforter as she got cozy.

"I should let you go."

"Just a little longer."

Since he wanted the same thing, he didn't say goodbye, just kept her on the line, talking about nothing important and feeling all the hard, brittle pieces of himself settle back into place.

But she yawned at least three more times.

So, he knew he had to let her get some sleep.

"I should—"

Pounding on his front door.

The bell going.

And then again.

And then *again*.

And...more pounding.

Jordyn's voice was alert when she asked, "What's that?"

"It's nothing," he assured her.

The pounding increased in volume.

"I should go."

"Ben—"

More doorbell and...it sounded like Maddy—because who else?—was slamming something against the door, battering ram style.

Christ.

"I'll see you tomorrow."

"But—"

"*Tomorrow,* sweetpea."

Then he hung up, got dressed, shoved his phone in his pocket, his feet in shoes.

Down the stairs.

Ripping open the front door.

Maddy was tripping, out of her fucking mind...and slamming a wooden pot that had formerly held flowers against the door.

Soil was all over the porch.

The flowers were trampled.

And because he'd surprised her by opening the door, now dirt had been sprinkled into his hallway.

Onto his rug.

Onto his floor.

And—he snapped.

Slamming the door behind him, he hit the button on the keypad to lock it, the dents on the freshly painted surface sparked his fury further. He ripped the pot from her hand, throwing it to the side, then gripped her arm.

"Benny?" A sad, quiet question.

He didn't say a word.

Not one *fucking* word.

And she unleashed on him. "Don't look at me like that. It's *your* fault I'm like this. *Your fault!*"

The last was a scream.

The last...

Settled on him, a heavy mantle of truth.

All this guilt.

All this beating himself up.

All this trying to fix her, fix his mom, keep things together.

And for what?

It was always going to come down to this.

He was the only one in the equation never doing enough.

He shook her slightly, enough to get her unfocused eyes to come to his. "Enough," he gritted out. "People are trying to sleep."

"I don't give a fuck!"

Striving for calm even though his anger had boiled over like an erupting volcano, he dragged Maddy to his car, shoved her in the passenger's seat.

A breath.

Control.

It was always going to be like this.

It was never going to change, never going to be that he'd done enough, and—

Why?

Why did he keep doing it?

He didn't have a good answer by the time he got in the driver's seat. Because guilt and a sense of duty both weren't cutting it any longer.

Why was *he* the only one to blame?

Keys in the ignition, engine on, locks engaged, pulling out of the driveway.

"You're such a fucking asshole! Always got to have what Ben wants, don't you? Always—"

What he wanted?

Fuck, besides hockey and until Jordyn, he couldn't remember a time he'd taken what he'd wanted.

Always, *always* his first focus had been Maddy and his mom.

"Always so fucking selfish, aren't you?!" she screamed, kicking out at his dashboard, totally fucking high and out of control. "You don't give a fuck that I'm suffering—"

That temper he'd managed to rein in snapped again.

"You think I don't give a fuck?" he screamed. "You think *I* don't give a fuck? I paid every bill, made every meal. I did laundry and got you to school. I made sure Mom was up and going to work so there was money for clothes and bills and food. And when there wasn't?" He yanked the steering wheel, pulled over to the side of the road. "*I* was the one who didn't eat. *I* was the one who wore too-small clothes and shoes. So yeah, I got a fucking scholarship to go to school, to get the fuck out. I took it. You were *fourteen*. You should have been able to manage. I did at *eight*, for fuck's sake."

"I shouldn't have had—"

"Of fucking course not," he snapped, slapping his hands on the steering wheel. "Mom should have been able to take care of you. But what would you have had me do? Quit school? Not play hockey when I made the team? You know how hard I struggled to play at all after Dad left, how difficult it was to get to games and afford equipment. And then I had a chance to go to a school with a team I might *make?*" He turned to face her. "I got a scholarship from *one* college, Mads. One. If I didn't take that chance, I knew I wouldn't have another."

"That's bullshit," she said, eyes bruised but clearing, the drugs wearing off. "You wanted to get out."

He sighed. "Of course I did! I wanted to do one thing for *me*. One thing for *my life*. Does that make me a selfish asshole? Yes. I guess it does. At least according to you and Mom." He sucked in a breath. "But I was trying to get a better life for me, for *us*. I never left you behind. Even then I was checking in, I was sending money. I didn't party with the guys because my whole focus was getting good grades and playing as well as I could and taking care of you both."

"But you weren't here."

That was the crux of it.

That was the piece he could never change.

"No," he said. "I wasn't."

"And because of that—"

His patience was gone. His normal filter for the sister he'd loved, the sister who wasn't this woman, had disappeared.

"At some point you have to stop blaming me for the fucked-up decisions you made in your life," he snapped. "At some point you have to take responsibility for your own fucked-up shit. Because I'm not always going to step in, Maddy. I'm done. I'm tired. I want you to get better, but only you—"

She wound up like she was going to hit him.

He caught her wrist. "*Don't.*"

Fury in her eyes, angry tears sliding down her cheeks. She yanked out of his grip then moved so quickly he was left flat-footed. One second she was trying to hit him, the next she was scrabbling at the door handle, wrenching open her side, jumping out of the car.

Fuck.

He threw the car in park, struggled with his belt.

And by the time he rounded the car, searching the busy San Franciscan streets, he'd lost sight of her.

TWENTY-FIVE

JORDYN

It was nine-fifteen.

The car was loaded.

Ben's sandwich had joined the others in the cooler.

Josh and Jess were running behind but due any moment with Amelia and all her necessary baby gear.

The boys were hopped up on homemade donuts.

But Ben wasn't there.

And he'd sent no word.

No text. No email. No call from Ben. And he hadn't returned any of hers either.

Worry was clawing its way through her belly, digging in to stay for the long haul after another message and call went unanswered when Josh and Jess pulled into the driveway.

Josh got out, reaching into the back for the car seat and rounding the hood with it in hand.

Jess gathered her bag, started to get out, but froze when she turned in Jordyn's direction. "What's the matter?" she asked quickly, hustling over to her.

"Your auntie is coming—" Josh went still, too, seemingly just now taking in Jordyn's face. "Jor?"

God. Did she really look that bad?

Considering she'd been up all night, worrying, worrying so much that she'd almost gotten the kids out of bed and driven to Ben's, she supposed she *did* look that bad.

"I'm okay," she said.

Josh carefully set the car seat down. "No, you're not."

She wasn't. She was *worried.*

But she was okay.

"I'm fine," she said, putting her hand up when Josh opened his mouth to argue. "It's Ben."

Her brother blew out a breath. "Ben's good. I just texted with him."

"When?" And yeah maybe the question was sharp.

"Yesterday evening," he said, pulling out his phone, scrolling through the messages. "Look. See? He asked me if I had the updated travel details for next week."

They had texted.

"No," she said, shoving it back. "We were talking last night after that and there was a bunch of noise in the background. He told me it was fine, that it was nothing. But he hung up quick, and then he was supposed to be here." Fuck. She should have called the police or Josh or someone to go over instead of lying in bed worrying and being altogether useless. "But he didn't reply to my messages and he didn't pick up and"—she nibbled at her lip— "he's not here when he said he was going to be."

Josh glanced away from her, locked gazes with Jess.

"He's not with another woman," Jordyn said. "It's—" Was she really going to tell her brother she was fucking his teammate? "It was like pounding on the door, like someone was trying to break in."

"Call him," Jess said, scooping up Amelia's seat and nodding toward the porch.

Josh hesitated but followed her, his phone to his ear.

Anxiety was creeping through her veins, sitting heavy on her lungs, collapsing heavier when Josh frowned, pulling his phone away from his ear and glancing at the screen.

He typed out a text.

They all waited.

Then he dialed again.

Nothing.

Hesitation was replaced by worry on her brother's face. "We'll figure it out, Jor," he murmured. "Promise."

Then he called Brit, asked her to phone Ben.

She got no response either.

The boys came out, and she tried to plaster on a happy expression, but she failed miserably at it. Luckily, Jess took the lead, distracting them with a new plan to go for donuts before the beach, but not wanting to move Amelia's car seat. That got them into motion, busying the boys with moving all the beach stuff from their van to Jess and Josh's SUV and sweeping them out of there before they could discern Jordyn's—and now *Josh's*—worry.

"Keep me posted, yeah?" Jess said after checking to make sure everyone was buckled in.

"Yeah," Jordyn agreed. "But the boys...you don't have—"

"They're excited to go, and I'm fine." A smile. "Promise."

Jordyn nodded, thanking her, then turned back to her brother. "What do you—" Her phone rang and she nearly dropped it, just trying to extract it from her pocket. "It's him," she said, quickly swiping across the screen. "Ben. Oh my God. Are you—"

"I need you, sweetpea."

His voice didn't sound like him.

Not at all.

But she didn't focus on that.

"Where?" she asked, knowing that the first step was getting to him.

"My house."

"I'll be there in ten minutes."

"Jor?" Josh asked when she hung up. "He's—" A shake of her head, moving toward the front door. "He doesn't sound right." She grabbed her purse and keys off the table, locked up. "He's at his place and—"

She broke off, swallowed hard.

Josh squeezed her shoulder. "Later," he said. "For now, let's just get there."

———

His porch was...a fucking mess.

Littered with dirt, the large wood pot that had been full of flowers the last time she'd been there was dumped on its side and malformed.

The front door was damaged, deep grooves were dug in the wood.

But the man who was sitting on the steps was what really made her skin prickle.

"Ben!" She ran over to him, kneeling in front of him.

His head came up, eyes haunted.

"What, honey?" she asked softly, reaching for his limp hands.

"Maddy."

For a second, the name threw her. Then she realized, "Your sister?"

He nodded. "She came by last night, high or drunk or"—he waved a hand at the mess covering the porch—"or both. She—"

That haunted look crowded into his beautiful eyes. "She said it was my—"

He broke off, but she had a feeling she knew how he would have finished that statement. "Then what happened?"

"I was taking her back to the rehab and we fought and—" His eyes went a little glassy. "And she jumped out of the car." He explained how she'd run from him, run through the busy streets, getting lost in the crowd, how he'd walked the city all night looking for her. "I couldn't—" His words stoppered up again and he stared down at his hands. "I couldn't find her."

"We'll get the guys together, start a search," Josh said, making Jordyn jump.

She'd been so focused on Ben, she'd almost forgotten he was there.

"There's no point." Ben shook his head sharply. "If she doesn't want to be found, she won't be."

"We can still look," she told him.

His eyes on hers, guilt and worry and frustration all mixed together.

"Did you call your mom?" she asked gently. "Maybe she went to her house since she couldn't hang out here?"

"No." A breath. "I didn't call her. My mom would just—it would be too much for her. And Maddy doesn't go back to *that* house. Not ever."

The emphasis on *that* told Jordyn enough.

That was where the bad things had happened. *That* was the place Maddy would avoid at all costs.

"Okay," she said. "So we start from where we left off and we get whoever's free to help look." The last she said to Josh, who nodded at her and was pulling out his phone, ready to activate the Gold phone tree...or the text chain, or What's App or how ever those guys communicated nowadays.

But then Ben's phone rang.

He glanced down at it, eyes not seeming to recognize the sound, and she realized he was so torn up, so off his game that he hadn't realized she'd been calling either.

Hadn't realized that *any* of them had.

He'd just...reached out to her because he needed her.

Heart squeezing hard, she picked up the phone, swiped across the screen to answer the call, and put it up to her ear. "Hello?"

She listened for a moment.

Then she handed it to Ben.

"It's the rehab facility."

Twenty-Six

Ben

He walked through the door and into the small bedroom that Maddy had been living in the last months.

His sister was sitting on the side of the bed.

And looking more clear-eyed than he'd seen her in years.

Years.

"Maddy girl," he said.

Her chin wobbled and then she was nibbling on her bottom lip, her eyes filling with tears.

He was across the room in an instant, sitting next to her on the bed, his arm around her shoulders. Half of him expected her to pull away, to be *that* Maddy again, the one who lashed out physically and emotionally.

The rest of him cracked.

Because she was shaking and clinging to his waist, repeating over and over again, "I'm sorry. I'm sorry."

"It's okay, honey. It's okay." And fuck if his own eyes weren't leaking, dripping hot tears down his cheeks, soaking into his shirt above where her tears were soaking into his middle. "We're okay. You're okay."

"I'm not," she whispered into his chest. "I'm so fucked up."

"This place can give you a chance to get better," he murmured, stroking a hand down her back. "If you're ready to let it."

Her silence in response hurt.

But before it really cut deep, she was pushing lightly against his hold, sitting up, sliding away from him.

"I know," she said and her eyes were on his again. Clear. Sober. The sister he'd loved, but the sister he hadn't really seen, not for years. "I know this place could be good for me." A sigh. "I've known that for a long time. I just..." Her lids slid down, breaking their eye contact, but not before he saw the tears glimmering in them. "I'm scared," she whispered. "So fucking scared that I'm going to do this, going to put the work in, that I'm going to *try*...and then at the end, I'm still going to be messed up."

He didn't know what to say to that.

It needed an answer, but he knew his instinctual one was wrong.

The words that bubbled up—a quick rebuttal of that statement, an assurance that she'd be "cured," an easy "Of course you're not going to still be messed up"—none of them were right.

That would discount the olive branch she'd just extended.

Crap on the hand she'd just extended.

So, he took a second. He took a breath.

He *thought*.

"I think it's okay to be scared," he whispered, snagging her hand, needing to touch her, needing her to know that he was there. "That means you care about the outcome."

Maddy went still next to him, her fingers convulsing tightly around his.

"And you're not messed up. Horrible things were done to you. You're struggling with that. *Anyone* would—"

"*Anyone* would get so fucked up that her brother looks pained every time he's near her?"

That was a bit convoluted, so it took him a moment to realize what she was saying.

And she was right.

"I *do* hurt when I see you," he admitted.

She flinched.

"But not because of you," he said. "Not you, Maddy girl," he murmured. "What he did to you, what you went through, what —" His voice cracked and he sucked in a breath, released it slowly. "The pain I have comes from me. I *wasn't* there. I *let* that happen. I—"

"No!" she spun to face him. "I shouldn't have said that. Not yesterday. Not *ever*. You were right. You spent so much time holding us together, I should have been able to handle it, should have—"

Guilt spun through him anew. "No one should have had to handle that, Mads. Not at fourteen. Not ever. In the car yesterday, I-I shouldn't have—*God*." He shook his head. "You were a *kid*. You were violated and alone and—"

"You were alone, too," she whispered. "And you were alone for years taking care of me and Mom. I should have been able to handle everything better. I should—"

He squeezed her hand. "I think I'm getting that we both wish that we did things differently."

A snort. "A lot fucking different. I"—she sighed—"I'm not sure I'm strong enough to not use when the memories crowd in, when th-they get—"

Fuck.

He gathered her close again, held her while those tears flowed, blinking back his own, knowing that this was another time where he didn't necessarily have the right thing to say, knowing that even if that was true, this was the most honest conversation he'd had with his sister in years.

Hating that it was here.

That it was about this shit.

But glad they were finally having a fucking conversation that didn't involve accusations and anger.

Tears and facing the pain of the past he could handle.

"Sorry," she whispered a few moments later. "I'm...I'm just a—"

He cupped her jaw. "You are who you are. And I love you."

Her breathing hitched again. "Don't make me cry again. God knows I've soaked your shirt enough already."

"Meh." He shrugged. "Cry away. Get it out. My shirt is damp already."

Her laughter was wet. But it was there and they were sitting calmly, talking about the past and the future and—

Her hand came to his arm, squeezed lightly. "I need you to know that I really am sorry for what I said—"

"You already apologized."

Now that hand covered his on her jaw, her eyes locking with his. "I'm sorry. I love you. I'm—I'm going to try, Benny. I really am."

"I'm here for you, anything you need, any step of the way."

Her eyes slid closed, pain written into the lines of her face. "I know." A breath and her lids peeled back, her fingers flexing on his. "But I need"—her throat worked, breath coming out in another shuddering exhale—"I need you to let me do this."

His brows pulled together.

But he didn't get a chance to ask her what she meant because she continued speaking.

"I need you to give me some space." Her mouth tipped up. "I'm sure you'll be happy to have a break from the middle-of-the-night visits."

"Mads..." he began.

Her hand slid away from his, lifting, smoothing over the furrow between his eyebrows. "I...I think I need to see that I can do this on my own, that whether I get sober or relapse, how I sort out my mind, how I find whatever happiness the universe wants to send my direction...I need to know all of that—" A breath, sharp and staccato. "I need to know that *I* can do those things on my own. I need to know that if I fail, I only have myself to blame."

His heart fucking *hurt.* "You're not alone."

"I know," she whispered, her eyes damp, but her voice gentle. "Just like I know that you'll be here when I make it through to the other side."

"But—"

How was he supposed to just let her do this on her own?

He'd spent the last years kicking himself for having not been here for her, for allowing everything that happened to her, and now she just wanted him to leave her alone.

"I know," she said, as though reading his thoughts. "But you were right last night, Benny. And it hurts knowing that I've hurt you. It hurts even more than the memories. It hurt even through the drugs. And I don't—I don't want to be this person anymore." She swallowed. "And the only way I know how to do that is to just fucking pull on my big girl pants and start doing it on my own."

It made sense.

He still hated every word she was telling him.

But he didn't tell her that, didn't push.

Instead, he drew her in for another long, tight hug and said, "I'll be here for you when you make it to the other side."

Her hand settled over his heart, just like it used to when she was little and he was soothing some nightmare she'd had.

It felt...right.

It felt like they were finally moving forward.

And when she whispered, "I know," he *knew* they were moving forward.

TWENTY-SEVEN

JORDYN

He walked out of the rehab looking like he'd been pulled backward through a hedge.

He walked out the doors toward her, not saying one word.

But his eyes were glued to hers and he was moving toward her.

Not stopping.

Not stopping until he was in her space, until his arms were coming around her, until he was encasing her in a tight hug that nearly stole every bit of her breath.

"Ben," she whispered.

He shuddered.

"Are you okay?"

A shake of his head.

So she just held on tight, thankful that she'd dropped Josh back at her house on the way, so that he could give Jess some help with the kids. Thankful that it was just her and Ben and that she could hold him for as long as it took for him to pull himself back together.

It took a long time.

But she wasn't impatient, didn't want him to hurry.

He'd held *her* while she broke down. The least she could do was return the favor.

Eventually, though, his grip loosened and he straightened away from her, somehow became a big, brawny hockey player again.

"I'm sorry," he said, throat working, eyes seeming to deliberately avoid hers.

"You have *nothing* to apologize for," she told him. "Nothing," she repeated. His gaze came back to hers, stark, but there was a bit of hope at the edges that had her asking, "How is she?"

Silence.

A long, slow exhale.

"She's better than I've seen her in years." Another sigh. "Last night, when we fought, I thought I'd lost her forever, but...it seems like it finally got through."

"That's good though, honey," she said. "Sometimes we don't want to change until everything really hits home."

A nod. "Yeah."

"So what's eating at you?"

"She wants to do it on her own."

Jordyn frowned. "She wants to leave the rehab?" That seemed like a really bad idea, an addict trying to get sober with no support.

"No," he said. "She wants to stay here. She just...doesn't want me visiting anymore. Doesn't want my mom to come either. She said she wants to prove that she can do it, that succeed or fail, it's on her shoulders."

That sounded different.

Hard.

But maybe the right thing to move forward, though Jordyn was nowhere near an expert.

"Are you going to let her do that?"

"I don't think I have a choice."

That was probably true…and another thing that sounded like it was going to be hard as hell.

He stroked a hand through her hair. "She said it's not my fault."

Jordyn inhaled sharply through her nose. "That's good, baby."

"I—" His eyes were a little lost when they came back to hers. "How do I believe her?"

Heart squeezing tightly, she wrapped her arms around his middle. "You do what she asked," Jordyn whispered. "You give her the space she needs, and then you're there for her when she's ready."

"Fuck." A harsh whisper.

She squeezed him tighter.

"I hate this."

"I know." She lifted on tiptoe, pressed a kiss to his jaw. "You like to fix things. But you can't fix this."

His sigh was frustrated and long.

But it came from love.

"Yeah," he eventually agreed.

She waited to see if he wanted to talk further, but when he fell silent, mind a million miles away, she bundled him into her car, buckled him in.

And then she took him home.

———

"How are you going to get the Falcon home?" Sammy asked.

Ben blinked, glancing up from the directions.

He'd been his normal self with the boys, albeit a bit quiet after the events of the last day. She knew he had to be tired, but when she'd offered to drive him back to his place—as she'd done earlier that afternoon (something that had ended with him asking her to wait while he changed his clothes then coming down the stairs with the barely begun Lego Millennium

Falcon in a big plastic tub)—he'd asked if it was okay for him to stay.

Okay?

She was hoping he would stay forever.

But she hadn't told him that, not right then, not after all that had gone down over the last day.

Later, she could tell him that.

"Ben?" Sammy asked.

Ben's gaze drifted toward hers, intense enough to make her breath catch. "Well, it might have to live here then." A beat and her heart felt like it had grown to three times the size. "If that's okay with your mom."

She exhaled, and it was shaky.

"Mom?" Sammy asked, turning toward her and giving her full-on puppy eyes.

He didn't need to wield that particular method.

Not at all.

"Yes," she said softly.

Because it would always be yes.

For the first time since she'd pulled into his driveway that morning, she saw the light reenter his eyes. He didn't comment on everything that was flowing between them beneath the surface, just nodded at her, his lips turning up slightly at the corners.

"Cool!" Sammy shouted, his casted arm nearly taking out all the progress they'd made on the giant spaceship that would apparently be taking up space in her house.

Because she was a sucker.

Because it would make her boys happy...and because those boys now numbered three.

———

"I should go home," he whispered, his arm wrapped tight around her shoulders.

They were sitting on the back deck, cuddled into a chair that should have only fit one person, and certainly only one big, bulky hockey player.

But they'd managed to squeeze themselves in.

And, truthfully, she preferred being plastered against his big, hard body than having her own chair.

Tough life.

She smothered a giggle and burrowed closer, burying her face into his throat. "No, thank you."

He chuckled then, a little rough, a little quiet.

But there.

"No, thank you?" he asked. "That's all you have to say?"

She nodded, tightened her arms that were wrapped around his middle. "Yup."

"I could stay a little longer."

"Or," she said, "you could come inside and watch a movie."

"It's late. The boys—"

"Are dead asleep and could stay that way through a tornado."

His arm around her tightened, his other hand smoothing down her back. "I don't want—"

"Just a little longer," she whispered. "Please."

He didn't fight her after that.

He didn't fight her as she rose from his lap, took his hand, and drew him inside.

He didn't fight her when she stopped outside her bedroom door, nor when she led him through it.

And when she reached for the hem of his shirt, tugging it up and over his head, when she bent and pressed a kiss to the spot on his chest above his heart...

He stopped with the not-fighting and started *moving*.

Hands wrapping around her waist, yanking her flush against his body. His mouth descending before the gasp even fully left her lips. One second she was pressed to him, the next she was in his arms and he was carrying her to her bed.

"I'm not going to say I should go," he said, setting her on the mattress and smoothing his palm down her front—along her throat, between her breasts, over her stomach.

"Good." It was breathless, but then his touch was *oh so close* to all of the parts she wanted him to stroke.

But he didn't touch them, not then.

Instead, he straightened...

And headed for the door.

Twenty-Eight

"I thought you said you weren't going to—"

He shut the door.

Flicked the lock.

"—leave," she finished on a whisper.

Spinning back, he took in the fucking breathtaking beauty of her—sprawled out on the mattress, elbows propping herself up, hair a bit mussed, expression...going from confused to heated.

"Oh," she said as he stalked toward her.

Today she'd been...

His rock. Thinking about *him*. Never letting him doubt for one moment that she was right by his side, that she would help him, that she'd be there for him.

Even when shit got real.

Even when it got fucked up.

So, yeah, it was late, and yeah, her boys were down the hall (hence the locked door), and yeah, she'd seen him in a fucked-up situation, but she'd led him to her bedroom and looked at him like he was the only thing she wanted on the planet.

And that felt...

Well, fuck if it wasn't the best thing ever.

He stopped by the bed, sat on the side of the mattress, and reached for her feet.

"What—" Her question stoppered up when he peeled off her fuzzy socks, when he began massaging the sole of her foot. "Oh," she said again. "That's—"

Her head flopped back onto her pillow, eyes sliding closed, lips parting on a moan.

"That's really, really good."

Would he rather her be moaning that when he was stroking into her?

Yes.

For fucking *sure.*

But she'd brought him back. She'd made him feel good.

So, the least he could do was return the favor.

And since Jordyn was turning into a puddle of goo just from him giving her a foot massage, he was in no hurry to rush this. Stroking the ball of her foot, the heel, each of her toes, taking it up to her ankle, her calf before switching sides, giving her other foot the same treatment.

Tracing his hands over her shins, along the outsides of her thighs and then sliding them in, dipping them into the waistband of her leggings.

She shivered, lids peeling back, revealing eyes that were full of heat, full of need.

His own body responded in kind, heat trailing down his spine, sinking into his belly, drifting lower.

Then she lifted her hips slightly.

Grinning, he took the unspoken demand to heart, tugging her leggings down, drawing them off her feet and tossing them to the side.

"Fuck," he muttered, "I can't wait to have these legs around me."

She nibbled at her bottom lip. "I—" He watched her battle the insecurity, watched her—respect coiling through his middle—tuck it away. A breath and then she sat up wrapped her arms around him. He knew it took courage for her to touch him, to be vulnerable and reach for him after that fucking ex of hers had been such an asshole to her. "Why don't you let me?"

He kissed her, slipping his tongue between her parted lips. "Because we have time."

Taking advantage of her sitting up, he reached for the hem of her shirt, tugged it up and over her head.

Fuck.

"You're so fucking beautiful," he whispered.

She shuddered, but whether it was the words or because he was slowly coaxing her back down to the mattress, he didn't know. He didn't care. She *was* beautiful and he *was* coaxing her back, trailing his hands over her body.

"These," he said, sliding his palms up, brushing a finger over the curve of her breast that was spilling out over the cotton of her bra. "*These* are designed to drive a man wild."

"Drive *you* wild," she murmured, reaching up and drawing his hand down, bringing it to her breast.

Her nipple was hard against his palm, a tempting furled bud that called to his fingers and tongue.

Slow.

Patience.

Showing this woman that he loved her. Showing this woman how much she meant to him. Showing—

"You're thinking so hard that it's making my brain hurt."

He jerked, fingers clenching on her breast.

Hard enough that he immediately loosened his hold, but that touch showed in her eyes. She'd liked it.

"You like it a little rough, sweetpea?"

A sharp inhale, her breast moving beneath his palm, dragging that hard nipple along his flesh, but though that had heat coiling tighter in his belly, desire nipping at his heels, his head spinning, her reaction to the question was answer enough.

"You do," he said, leaning forward, nipping at the underside of her jaw.

She gasped, fingers coming to his hair, holding him to her. "Apparently," she said on another gasp, while he used his teeth on her earlobe, dragging them down her throat. "I do like it a little rough."

Now it was his turn to inhale sharply.

He nipped her collarbone.

She jerked, nails digging into his arms, and his vision hazed red for a second, his hands shook as desire clawed its way through him. "What was that for?" she murmured, thighs spreading, making him almost desperate to crawl on top of her, to plunge deep and feel her wet and tight around his cock.

But control.

But slow.

But...exploring this bit of wicked, this bit of a little rough with her...that was more important.

"*That's* for giving me a raging hard-on." Need tearing through him, but he forced himself to keep his tone light as he pressed his teeth to the skin stretched taut over her other collarbone. "And *that's* for being so fucking sexy that you're undoing all my plans and making it hard for me to think."

She snaked an arm down between them, down his torso, down to his cock.

Before he could pull away, turn it back to her and *her* pleasure (and, it had to be said, the pleasure *he* got from seeing her cheeks flush, her eyes go molten, her body instinctively seeking his), her fingers tightened.

Tightened enough that he saw stars.

"I want you on top of me."

He was moving before he considered that it was going to unravel all his intentions, all his control, all his plans to take his time to make love to her, to undo her inch by luscious inch, to worship her with fingers and lips and tongue.

He was thinking about her tight, wet heat.

He was desperate to be inside, to feel her clamping down on him.

He was—

Well, frankly, he was struggling to remember why he'd had all those intentions in the first place, especially when her hand began stroking him through his pants, firm and fast.

"That's better," she murmured.

And he had the feeling that he'd just lost all that precious control he'd been struggling to hold on to.

Then that feeling became a certainty.

As in, he was certain that he'd lost all semblance of control.

Her thighs spread and her legs wrapped around him, trapping that hand still tightly gripping his dick, still stroking, between them.

No.

Only one leg wrapped around him.

The other had bent, Jordyn pressing her foot into the mattress, pushing against him.

Pushing him...over.

And suddenly his back was flush against the comforter...

And Jordyn was straddling his middle.

And...yup.

He'd totally lost control of this situation.

He normally liked to plan things out, to know the next steps, to have everything lined up properly in his mind.

It helped him stay focused, stay on course.

When he'd been a hockey player clawing his way through the ranks, that type of control had been necessary to corral his anxiety, to cope with the high stakes of his journey, especially with everything happening at home when that all blew up.

Now, he had his coping strategies.

Now, he could deal.

But he still liked to abide by his mental checklist, the neatly organized queue in his mind.

Him being pressed to the mattress, Jordyn's half naked body on top of his wasn't in the queue.

But he found that he didn't give *one* fuck.

TWENTY-NINE

JORDYN

She felt like she'd just climbed a mountain.

Was planting her flag at the peak.

And she knew she was smiling like a dope.

At least until Ben ratcheted up, slammed his lips to hers, slipped his tongue into her mouth, stroking fast and deep.

Smiling was suddenly the last thing on her mind.

She wanted him inside—wait.

No.

Well, *yes*, she definitely wanted that, definitely wanted to feel that slow burn as he pressed into her, the hard, hot heat, the strength of him, the size of him.

She wanted Ben inside her.

But...she wanted him naked first.

She wanted to see him, to touch and lick and stroke him. She wanted to get over the slight bit of fear that was coiling in the back of her mind, the tiny bite of hesitation she still felt before touching him, before kissing and holding and *stroking* him.

To do that, she needed to *do* that.

To touch and hold and—

His lips tipped up as he tugged her hand free from between them, pressed a kiss to her palm. Then—see? that hesitation was still there—she held her breath as his eyes came to hers and he brought her hand to his chest.

His heart was pounding beneath her touch, but she only felt it for a moment before he was lying back down on the mattress, those lips curving further. "You look good up there, sweetpea."

Everything inside her relaxed.

Hands on her hips, fingertips hot and a little rough.

Now *her* lips curved.

Just as she liked it.

She sat back slightly, straddling the hard length of him, intending to reach for his shirt, to yank it up and off, to expose the expanse of skin she *needed* to get her mouth on.

But when she paused, reaching back to push her hair out of her face, he went rigid beneath her.

"Fuck, baby," he groaned, fingers tightening on her hips.

Ice in her veins. Had she done something wrong?

But when she looked down at him, it wasn't annoyance on his face, wasn't anger in his eyes. Oh, those hazel depths positively blazed, but it wasn't with rage. Desire flamed out, bright and needy and calling to her, to that last bit of insecurity coiled to strike in her belly and mind. He *liked* what he saw—no, he fucking *loved* it.

No hidden barbs about stretch marks or her body changing.

No stopping her from touching him, from giving and receiving and playing an active role instead of a fucking toy to be used.

Nothing but her and Ben and the fact that they liked each other, that they were attracted to each other.

It was like Luke was manning one of the Falcon's guns, like he'd just closed his eyes and used the force to strike true with that one-in-a-million shot, and that laser blast was flying through all of her veins and nerves and muscles and cells and destroying that insidious insecurity that Daniel had implanted inside her.

One blazing shot.

And...*boom!*

She was in pieces.

And when she found herself drawn back together, centered herself on the way Ben held her, how he looked at her and made her feel. When she looked inward, studying those pieces that had slotted themselves back together...she was whole in a way she wasn't sure she had ever been.

Which was why she stopped thinking, stopped focusing on those sections inside her.

She had her kind, sexy, and *big* in all the right places hockey player between her thighs, need etched into his face, into the hard length pressing against her.

No more fucking around.

No more wallowing in the past.

She'd finally gotten her freedom.

She wasn't going to squander it.

"I take it that you like when I'm playing cowgirl?" she teased, keeping her arms raised, her hands in her hair—since clearly he liked that—as she rocked herself back and forth, back and forth across his cock.

Teasing—him, her.

"You can play cowgirl any time you want," he said, his voice rough like gravel, his fingers flexing hard enough to give her that little bit of rough.

She shivered.

Then she focused.

Dropping her arms and reaching for his shirt, wrestling it up and over his head. His chest was...hell, it was a work of fucking art, pecs that she wanted to squeeze. His abs were well-defined, his torso cut and rippling with a strength that made her feel safe and desperate to touch and...wanting him to use a bit of that strength on her.

But first...it was her turn.

She smoothed her hands over those squeezable pecs, trailed

her fingers over his abs, tracing every divot, every taut line of muscle. Her hands were followed by her lips, her tongue, tasting every inch, every hard bit of his strength. Until he seemed to lose control and his hand wove its way into her hair, tugging her up his body, sprawling her out on top of him. All of him pressed to all of her.

It was *glorious.*

Then his mouth was on hers, his kiss sending her pulse thundering in her veins.

It would be easy to fall into that kiss, into his hold, to let him take over. But she wasn't done with him yet. She needed more.

Managing to tear her mouth from his by pure dint of character, she slid down his body before he could stop her, mind on one thing and one thing only.

He was wearing sweats, gray and clingy and currently stretched to maximum capacity around his erection.

And she was thanking the hockey gods that he was wearing those sweats—not only because he was hot as fuck in them, but also because her hands were trembling so badly, her body so ratcheted up with need and desire that she wouldn't have been able to operate a zipper, wouldn't have been able to open a button.

But elastic she could manage.

Elastic could be tugged down to his strong, powerful thighs—something she did right then. Elastic could be freed from around his hard cock.

Elastic meant that she was free to bend down and suck him deeply into her mouth.

"Fuck!"

Her eyes shot up, mouth staying in place, but all she found in his was a burning need. For her. She worked her tongue, firmed her lips, put her hand into play, blowing him hard and fast and deep enough to have tears forming.

His curses were plentiful. His body taut and sheened with sweat.

But he didn't stop her, didn't force her head down or buck his hips up. He didn't do anything except weave his fingers into her hair and gently rest his palm on her head. Touching her, keeping that contact, but letting her lead.

Already, her appetite for leading was fading, decreasing as the dampness between her thighs increased.

But she *fucking* loved that she could make him feel like that, loved that he was close to the edge, loved that—

His fingers slipped from her hair, went to her shoulder.

Then she was drawn up his body again, plastered against his chest, which was heaving. "Fuck, honey," he rasped. "I—" He shifted them so he could look at her, and the smile he gave her was pure sin. "You can do that any time you want. *Any* time."

Now she was back to grinning. "You know you've just unleashed a monster?"

"*You* know that monster wants to blow me at regular intervals?"

She giggled.

And...laughing in bed was not something she'd ever expected. This push-pull of closeness, of intimacy and need, of give and take was not something she'd ever thought she wanted. It was different and...it was perfect.

Because it was the two of them.

"Well," she said, stroking her fingers along his jaw. "This monster thinks that she's ready for a little bit of rough." She leaned down, nipped his bottom lip. "Think you can manage to give that to—*ah!*"

THIRTY

"*Ah!*" she squeaked when he rolled them over.

A moment to kick off his sweats, another to reach beneath her and unclasp her bra.

"Thank fuck," he muttered, cupping her breasts and burying his face in them, rubbing his cheeks along the soft globes.

"Ben—"

"You don't like it?" he asked, flicking out his tongue, tasting one side and then the other.

A giggle. "I don't think I've been motorboated before."

Fuck, this woman undid him.

Made him happy and whole and loved.

"What's the verdict?" he asked softly, kissing his way up one breast, stopping just shy of one nipple.

"Ve-verdict?" she whispered.

"Did you like it?" He sucked her nipple between his lips, flicking his tongue over the hard bud.

She moaned.

He released her nipple, kissed his way to the other side. "Sweetpea?"

Her eyes came to his, glazed over and unfocused and, fuck, if pride didn't shimmer down his spine.

"Did you like it?"

A shake of her head. "Li-like?" Another shake, those eyes clearing enough to go soft, to give him all that warmth she had inside. "I like everything you do, baby."

He felt that *baby* in his dick.

And as quick as lightning streaking across the sky, desire leaped up and gripped him in its teeth, shaking him fiercely. Her other nipple had been neglected, so he cupped her breast, drew her nipple between his lips, and reveled in the way she lit up for him.

The way her moans echoed through the room, how her hands clenched on his shoulders, nails biting into skin, her hips working against him, back arching, offering herself up to him so freely that he had to reach down between them—mouth still on her breast—and slide his fingers through all that liquid heat of her.

Circling her clit, stroking in exactly the pattern he'd learned she liked.

Then pressing a finger into her, collecting her gasp on his tongue, tasting the pleasure he brought her, stroking her up, coaxing her toward the edge.

"Ben," she said, tearing her mouth from his and sucking in air. "*Ben—*"

"Yeah, sweetpea?"

"Inside me. Please."

He wanted to make her come first. He wanted—

Her hand wrapped around him, positioned him at her entrance, stroking him through all that hot, wet heat.

Yes.

Inside.

He wanted that.

The tip of his cock caught on a downward stroke and notched itself at her entrance.

Fuck yeah, he wanted that.

He *needed* it.

Except—

"*Shit.* Condom. Baby, I don't have—" For fuck's sake. He was a grown man.

He needed to sort out birth control.

"Nightstand," she said. "I grabbed some after—" She was rubbing herself against him. "Last—" Another rub, all those glistening folds against his cock. "After last—"

She broke off again, but he was already moving, already fishing out the box of condoms, tearing the cardboard and yanking out a plastic square. A second later, he had the packet open and was rolling it down his cock, all while that glistening pussy lay spread wide and bare for him.

Then he was stroking in and he wasn't going gentle or slow, wasn't in control in the least.

He was giving her that little bit of rough.

He *couldn't* finesse this.

It was all-encompassing and intense and—

So many things that he couldn't begin to name them, to tease them apart, to separate sensation from thoughts and categorize them into actual words.

It was just *them.*

Pleasure coiling in his belly, warning bells going off, knowing he was going to come and he was going to do it soon and that unless he got her there with him really quickly, he was going to do that alone. So, he brought his hand between them, giving her that little bit of rough on her breasts, on her nipples, bent, slanting his mouth, taking that rough into their kiss, into the way he was thrusting hard and fast and deep.

It was a double-edged sword, yanking him closer and closer to the edge, playing with fucking fire.

But thankfully, her hips started bucking against his, meeting him stroke for stroke.

Her head pressed back into the pillow, breaking the kiss, arching on the mattress.

"Oh shit," she whispered. "Oh shit, oh shit, oh *shit!*"

And, thank fuck, he felt her starting to convulse around him.

His orgasm was already there, barreling down on him, and... he exploded.

Wave after wave of pleasure careened through his body, his strokes got erratic, his vision hazed, and...

...he came to collapsed on top of her.

"Shit. Sorry, sweetpea," he said, rolling them to the side, tucking her close against him.

She rubbed her face against his chest. "I don't mind getting squished by you."

"Good," he murmured, stroking a hand down her spine, letting it drift back up.

"Also"—she leaned back enough to meet his gaze—"motorboating for the win."

He was still breathing heavy, but he'd already had the biggest smile on his face. He could actually feel it creasing his cheeks, it was so freaking giant. Her words though? They had laughter bubbling up, exploding out to fill the room, weaving through the space to tangle with hers.

This woman.

God. He loved her.

A noise prickled through the heavy sleep that was weighing down his eyelids, his brain slowly coming to attention.

He'd been so tired after everything that had happened, and especially after the orgasm that had nearly sheared him in half, that he must have fallen asleep.

It was Jordyn's scent in his nose, Jordyn's lush body pressed to his.

Peeling open his eyes, he glanced down and smiled.

Yup.

His Jordyn curled up against him.

Yeah, all was right in the world.

She moaned softly, burrowing into him.

Tightening his arms, he let his eyes slide closed again. Tired. He was still tired, and holding a naked Jordyn in his arms was the perfect way to get more rest.

Except...there was that noise again, prickling through his senses.

He opened his eyes again, frowning, listening hard, more awake than asleep now.

But the house was quiet.

Sighing, he settled back into the pillows, started to go back to sleep—

"Hey, Jor! We're here to pick up the boys!"

Josh's voice.

Josh.

Jordyn's brother's voice.

Her *brother.*

"Jor!" A knock. "You still sleeping?"

She was.

But not for long.

"Jordyn," he said, shaking her until her eyes began to open. "Jor. Honey." He shook her a little harder. "Your brother is—"

Right on the other side of the locked door.

And Ben was naked. In bed and naked with his *sister.*

Shit. *Shit.*

"Jor!"

She finally went alert, jerking up to sitting, clutching the sheet to her chest.

"Your brother is—"

The knob jiggled.

It was locked.

They were good.

They were—

The knob *turned.*

The door opened.

And then he was face-to-face with Jordyn's brother.
Fucking *hell*.

Thirty-One

JORDYN

Everything happened in an instant.

One second, she was happily snuggled into all the yummy warmth that was Ben.

The next, she was awake and naked and trying to puzzle together Ben's urgent words.

Before she could do that, Josh was standing in the doorway of her room, Jess right behind him, Amelia perched on her hip, the door flung open, and—

Ben slid from the bed, snagging a pillow as he did, holding it in front of...well, all of the important bits. "Josh."

Another one of those strange moments in time, everything moving slow and then abruptly going really, really fast.

Josh was at the door.

Josh was in front of Ben, fists clenched at his side.

"It's not what you think," Ben said, which Jordyn had to admit, caused her to giggle hysterically.

(Definitely not the right thing to do in that moment when Josh looked ready to commit homicide...or Goldicide or—)

Another giggle.

"It's not what you think," Ben doubled down on. "Jordyn is—"

He didn't get to finish whatever explanation he thought was going to make this situation okay, whatever clarification it was he thought he could tell her brother that was going to smooth everything over.

Because Josh punched him.

Like just picked up his fist and socked Ben right in the face.

Ben grunted and went down hard enough to shake the floor.

For a moment, she was shocked, frozen, sitting up in bed, still clinging to the sheet, pressing the material tightly between her breasts.

Then that cold went molten hot.

Because Ben had picked himself—and the pillow—up, clamping the latter t to his groin, the former wavering slightly, his free hand coming up to cover his eye.

She could already see that it was bruising, and damn, it was swelling around his fingers.

Josh stepped forward, his fist lifting.

The molten fury inside her exploded.

Lurching to her feet—and luckily taking the sheet with her so as not to flash her brother and Jess—she marched around the side of the bed, shoving herself between her brother and her... boyfriend, lover, *everything*.

"Don't touch him!" she snapped.

A hand around her middle, tugging her back against a strong, warm chest.

Josh's eyes flashed. "Don't touch *her!*"

"Calm down, man," Ben said, though his voice was far from calm. Shocked again, she glanced up at him, at the man who'd just spoken with such deadly intent. A muscle in his cheek was twitching and his jaw was set in harsh lines.

"You fucking asshole," Josh growled. "*You* calm—"

Laughter, sudden and loud and full of absolute joy, filled the room.

Jordyn gaped at Jess, who was bent double in laughter, Amelia's babbling accompanied with a few giggles—probably because her mom was being a loon—and batting Jess's arms with her tiny fists. Totally flummoxed, she glanced away from Jess and her adorable niece and up at Josh and Ben—only to see they were giving her sister-in-law the same exact bewildered expression that must certainly be on her own face.

"What?" she asked when it seemed as though Jess was content to just continue laughing.

Jess froze, then straightened slowly, Amelia still having the time of her life, being held by her laughing mommy. Though, Jess's laughter cut off just as abruptly as it had begun. Then she just lifted her brows at Jordyn, as though expecting her to understand her amusement.

Jess pointed. "Do you *not* see the humor in this?"

Jordyn was running more than a little short on humor in the current situation. But she didn't say that. Instead, she clutched the sheet tight, raised her eyebrows in question to Jess, and then just slowly shook her head at Jess.

Who just grinned and said, "Think back to last year, and maybe your brother and I were found by your boys in a..." She paused long enough for her meaning to be clear. "*Similar...*" Emphasized as though Jordyn hadn't already remembered.

And how could she have forgotten, even for a second?

"...situation."

She'd come to visit, had played hooky from school for a few days, and had taken the boys down to Disney. But they'd made a pit stop at Uncle Josh's.

And the boys had decided to wake him up...which had ended up in waking *Jess* up.

Josh—and clearly the DNA was strong with the men in her family—had slept right through the boys' bum rush.

"This is hardly the same thing," she snapped.

Jess smirked. "Feels like it kind of might be."

She would not be amused. She *would not* be amused. She would not—

Jess's smirk widened.

But she didn't comment further, just propped Amelia up a little higher on her hip and walked across the bedroom—across her former bedroom—and plunked her daughter into Josh's arms. Then she began tugging him from the room, drawing him out into the hall, pulling the door closed behind her.

Then she went back to commenting (and smirking widely). "Sorry about the"—a nod at the door—"we thought you might be stuck because of the wonky lock on the knob." A flutter of her hand. "We'll just leave you two to…" Another flutter that had Jordyn close to wanting to throttle her sister-in-law (mostly because she was filling Jordyn's belly with amusement and Jor was having a hell of a time holding it in…and *this was not the time* to start busting up, contrary to Jess's actions). "To make yourselves presentable," Jess finished.

The door *clicked* closed.

But even with the wood between them, Jordyn could still hear Jess laughing her head off as she made her way down the hall.

Sighing, she turned to Ben, wincing at the state of his eye already. "I'm—"

A finger laid across her lips, silencing her apology.

She'd expected anger or regret or…something that wasn't the edge of humor treading through the swirling gold and brown and green of his eyes. "Wonky doorknob?"

Another wince. "I—"

His lips tipped up, and hell if he didn't look ridiculous smiling like that while standing there with a pillow clenched to his junk, his black eye blooming darker by the second. Then he dropped the pillow, wrapped his arms around her, and tugged her close.

Inconveniently, her belly tingled with desire.

"Why do I want you still?" she whispered.

His smile widened. "That's a bad thing?"

"It's a bit ill-timed"—great, now she was the one who was smiling—"don't you think?"

He brushed his knuckles over her cheek. "No, sweetpea," he said. "You wanting me is never a bad thing. No matter the timing."

"Why am I suddenly getting the urge to push that and find a time when it is?"

A rough chuckle. Another brush of his knuckles. "You could never inconvenience me." A beat. "And I love that you're comfortable enough with me to show me that hidden vein of sass."

Warm in her eyes. "I hope you know what you're getting yourself into."

"I know," he murmured. "And I'll treasure it every second of every day."

She inhaled sharply, those words undoing her.

She wanted to kiss him. She wanted to *fuck* him.

But her brother was waiting in the kitchen and she was still naked.

Sigh.

Stepping away from him, she moved to her dresser, began pulling out clothes, both disappointed and relieved when Ben started retrieving his clothes from where they lay scattered about the floor and tugging them on.

Though it was a shame that the man was covering up that ass.

She wanted to bite it.

She wanted—

"Dressed, sweetpea."

Realizing she was still clinging to the sheet, the underwear she'd set out still sitting on top of her dresser, she shimmied into her panties, clipped her bra around her middle and then tucked away the girls.

Sweats. A T-shirt.

Socks because her feet always got cold on this hardwood floor.

Ben was dressed by the time she managed with that, and she couldn't lie, when he moved to the opposite side of the mattress and helped her make up the bed without a word, without having to be asked, she fell in love with him even more deeply.

Because that small gesture was Ben to a T.

Walking around the bed brought her into his path, into his arms. She reached up, gently touched the spot beneath his injured eye. "Does it hurt very much?"

"You're worried about a guy who stands in front of hundred-mile-per-hour hockey pucks?"

She smoothed her fingers down over his cheek. "I don't ever want to see you hurt."

A sharp inhale, his hands tightening on her waist, lips parting as though he'd say something—

Then pounding feet down the hall.

Excited boyish voices shouting, "Uncle Josh!" A moment later they heard, "Pancakes!"

Ben exhaled. "Saved by the children."

"Saved by the children," she agreed on a grin, taking his hand, drawing him from the room, down the hall, and into the kitchen where her brother was indeed preparing to make his famous—at least according to her boys—pancakes with real whipped cream and berries.

She got her hugs, and Ben got his greetings.

Josh and Jess set the kids to work, effectively distracting them with tasks so that her brother could draw her and Ben aside.

"What the fuck happened to going slow?" he snapped at Ben.

"Stop right there," she said, lifting a hand and cutting him off before he could spew any further protective older brother nonsense. "This isn't your life. This isn't your call. Ben and I decide the limits and parameters of what we have between us." A finger poking into his chest. "*We* decide. Not you."

Protest welling up in Josh's eyes.

She fixed him with a glare that had never once failed to make her boys behave.

Thankfully, it also worked on brothers.

Especially when paired with the truth.

"Daniel broke me," she whispered. "But Ben brought me back. Ben gave me the strength to want to try again."

Her brother stilled, jaw clenching.

But she knew she had him.

Because he'd seen her broken...and he was seeing her now.

"He brought me back," she repeated. "And I won't let anyone hurt him." A narrow-eyed look that melted the rest of the ice on his face, that sent guilt trailing in its wake. "Not *anyone*."

Jess leaned in, kissed Jordyn on the cheek. "Tell him, honey."

Josh sighed, glanced up at the ceiling. "Christ. Don't I get anyone on my side?"

"He makes her happy," Jess said, passing Amelia over to Ben. "And can't you see she does the same for him?"

A grumble.

But Josh didn't try to interject again, didn't play overprotective older brother.

He just sighed, extended his hand.

Ben shook it.

"You hurt her, I kill you. Teammate or not."

"Josh!" she and Jess exclaimed. So much for not playing the overprotective older brother.

"Fair enough," Ben agreed over their protests.

A grunt from her brother.

The handshake completed.

Josh went back to pancakes.

The atmosphere in the kitchen was tense. A little awkward. Far from perfect.

But that was okay. Real life was messy and a little awkward. Sometimes tense. Oftentimes far from perfect.

Plus, she considered it a victory when Josh didn't poison Ben's share of the pancakes.

Thirty-Two

BEN

He walked into the locker room, felt Josh's eyes laser right toward him.

Threatening to burn him to a crisp.

It was early.

They had practice today and a game tomorrow night...and then the rest of the season with lots of together time ahead.

And he was fucking Josh's sister.

Loving her, too, but since he hadn't told Jordyn that yet, he couldn't pass on that fun little tidbit. Yes, he was fully aware that mentally, at least, he was being ridiculous. But it was better than staring into the eyes that threatened to slowly peel the flesh from his body and then toss it onto the ice and skate back and forth over it.

Repeatedly.

Jordyn and Jess had run interference the day before.

Today...he was trapped in a locker room with the man.

Brit walked into the room, backpack on her shoulders, striding across the space to her stall, bag sliding free of her body, plunking onto the bench. But before she sat down, that long, lanky body of hers froze.

Unfortunately, while she was looking at him.

She straightened, reversed back across the room—literally reversed like she was a car backing down a driveway, not turning around, but walking backward until she was stopping right in front of his locker.

She whistled. "Benny, you've been keeping secrets."

A snort from Josh.

And that was all it took for Brit to put the pieces together.

"Joshie," she said in a voice loud enough that everyone in the half-filled—and filling more by the second—locker room stopped, focus arrowing right toward Josh. "Why ya punching our Benny?"

Swear to fuck—swear to *fuck*—Ben could almost hear those gazes swiveling toward him, a *whoosh* through the suddenly tensed air of the room. He saw more than one set of eyes go wide when they took in the bruise on his face.

Which he couldn't blame them for.

When'd he'd looked in the mirror that morning, he'd seen that his black eye had reached colors of truly magnificent proportions —purple and green and blue with hints of yellow and black.

It was a Jackson Pollack painting on his face.

Good times.

Josh's only response to Brit was a grunt.

But Brit was Brit, and she wasn't about to be dismissed with a mere grunt.

She spun to face Ben, lifted her brows, fixed him with that Brit Look that had caused greater men than him to crumble.

He held his tongue. Barely.

"Gonna keep your secrets, Benny?" she asked, a shark circling beneath him in an ocean of danger.

Because Josh's laser eyes had become...something more dangerous than lasers.

C-4? Missiles? Nuclear?

"Let's just get ready for practice, yeah?" he asked.

Plus, he probably needed to be prepared to be laid the fuck out by a certain defenseman.

"Practice." Brit sighed, but she let the topic drop, moving forward to her stall. "Fine," she muttered and it was definitely begrudging. "We'll get ready for practice."

Ben ignored it.

But then Josh snorted again and his temper that had been deeply banked because he had a sister who—despite all their issues—he felt very protective over, all of which meant that he understood where Josh was coming from, knew that he'd have been pissed as hell too if he'd found a man in his sister's bed. But that snort sent his temper from deeply banked to boiling. Set it gathering steam in his belly, his veins.

His hands squeezed into fists.

His jaw clenched.

He tried to bite back a response, but then Josh huffed and his irritation was so fucking...big, heavy, and *stifling* that Ben felt like he was fucking choking on it.

And that pissed him off, too.

Josh knew he wasn't a fucking douchebag trying to take advantage of his sister. Ben had made that clear before yesterday. And, hell, yesterday Jordyn had thrown down for him, too, had made it clear that Ben made her happy.

The boys liked him.

He liked them back. Hell, he was growing to love them as much as he loved their mother. They were great kids. What wasn't to love?

So he wasn't fucking around with Jordyn's heart.

He loved her. She loved him back—or he hoped that was the proper interpretation of the warmth in her eyes, the way she'd stood by him, how she'd told off her brother.

For *him.*

So Josh needed to just get the fuck over his being with Jordyn.

Ben wasn't going to give her up.

Which was probably why his temper exploded.

"Josh punched me because I'm in love with his sister."

The room—mostly filled now—went absolutely still. Even Brit. Her mouth dropped open, though she couldn't be surprised that he was interested in Jordyn. He'd been at her house, he'd been spending time with the kids.

They were all being *real* cool about not pushing him to explain that interest.

But the black eye couldn't be much of a shock considering that he hadn't been shy about showing that interest.

"No," Josh muttered, shoving his feet into his skates. "I punched you because I walked in on you naked in bed with my sister. You're still *alive* because you love my sister."

Someone whistled.

Someone else hissed out a breath.

Coop winced.

Brit was grinning.

Rome cursed under his breath.

"Lucky you're not fucking dead, bro," Logan said.

"Seriously," Kayden muttered.

"He's neglecting to mention the fact that he let himself into Jordyn's house and barged into her bedroom."

"I was worried she was trapped inside."

Now *Brit* snorted. "What? She doesn't know how to work a doorknob?"

"No," Josh snapped. "That doorknob is a little wonky and—" He sighed, rubbed his hand over his head. "Look. Should I have waited to go in? Yeah. But—"

"You were worried," Ben finished when he cut himself off. "I know," he said softly. "I get it."

The nukes in Josh's eyes disappeared and they were back to lasers.

Lasers that collided because Ben's temper wasn't completely cooled either.

But lasers that came to a nonverbal agreement.

Ben didn't hurt Jordyn.

Josh wouldn't hurt Ben.

It wasn't forgiveness for being naked in bed with his sister.

But he was all but giving Ben the green light to keep moving forward with Jordyn, *and* the relationship wasn't going to implode the locker room.

So it was good enough.

———

Fully dressed, he slipped out into the hallway, wanting to get on the ice.

Wanting to feel the cool air making his skin grow tight, feeling the rush as the ice crunched beneath his skates.

Wanting to just...*hockey*. For a few minutes.

No drills. No fancy footwork to warm up.

Just him and his stick. A puck and his equipment.

But as he turned to head out to the rink, he heard a noise. No. Not a noise. A conversation and though he couldn't actually discern the words they were exchanging, he could tell they were sharp, stilted, and—

He spun to look down the hall and saw Will standing very close to a woman Ben didn't recognize.

She was tall, slender, and her skin was tinted with gold.

Beautiful in an almost gentle way—even if that gentle didn't match with the conversation she was having with Will.

She rose on tiptoe, her nose so close to Will's that their faces were practically touching. Another sharp exchange and then she was brushing past Will.

Ben caught a glimpse of the Gold logo emblazoned above her heart and had a feeling who she was.

And perhaps, who she was to Will.

But he didn't want to get caught having been eavesdropping, so he spun quickly, focusing on the rack of sticks, concentrating on them like he was a sommelier trying to select the best bottle of wine. Footsteps closing in, moving beyond him in a rapid clip.

Disappearing around the corner to where the staff kept the offices.

Interesting.

"You're a shit eavesdropper, you know that, right?" Will muttered, coming up behind him.

"You're going to be late for practice if you don't get dressed."

"Nice try." A beat. "What'd you hear?"

"Hear?" Ben snagged his stick, spun to face Will. "Nothing."

Eyes narrowing, Will opened his mouth.

"Nothing except that you two were exchanging some sharp words I couldn't discern. But," he added, glancing up into his friend's stark face, "I saw—can *see*—that whatever it was she said sliced you to ribbons."

Will inhaled. Let the exhale out slowly. "I'm fine."

Sure he was. But Ben wasn't Brit. He wouldn't push—not right in that moment anyway. Not when Will looked fucking sick to his stomach.

"Who is she?" he asked instead.

"Lily Cartwright," Will said softly, and the name immediately triggered a blip of recognition though Ben couldn't remember why. "She's the sports psychologist that management just hired."

Right.

Ben had seen the email with her biography come through his inbox.

But he didn't think Will was so upset over a new hire.

"And who's she to *you?*" he asked quietly.

Will inhaled, let it out slowly, pain cutting through his eyes. *"Everything."*

THIRTY-THREE

She was wearing a fancy dress and heels and lingerie that she was hoping Ben would peel off her later.

The boys were at Josh and Jess's.

A date with Ben.

An actual date to a restaurant, which would be followed by canoodling at a movie.

Then it would be back to what had become their usual—Ben coming over after games, Ben hanging with the boys and her, eating dinner and playing games, her taking the boys to his place for a couple of hours, walking the trail behind his house (sans additional broken bones—though, thankfully, Sammy's cast was going to be coming off in the very near future). Squeezing in time because she had work and two boys and was dating a hockey player who was busy for half the week, either at the rink for practice or a game or on a plane heading *to* a game.

So she and Ben having time for just the two of them was a precious gift.

And she'd gone all out.

With lacy lingerie and a tight dress she never would have dared to wear before—not when she'd been so uncomfortable in her own body, her own mind. Not when she'd worried so much about what Daniel would think.

Now she *knew* what Ben would think, knew he loved her body, that he would take one look at the tight black material (with ruching in all the right places, deemphasizing her FUPA, drawing attention to the breasts he loved so much).

Thinking about how he'd worshipped them the last time he'd come over, sneaking her to her bedroom (with a new—and lock-able—doorknob) after the boys had gone to bed, thinking about how he'd nearly driven her to an orgasm just by kissing and licking and sucking and squeezing them had her cheeks flushing, her nipples beading against all that lace she was wearing.

She'd gotten so close to the edge with his ministrations that she was game to try again.

This time, though, she would control herself and not tackle her man back to the mattress and have her merry way with him.

Okay, probably not.

She had no self-control when it came to Ben.

Every time he was near, she wanted to rub herself against him like a cat.

But later.

Because she had a surprise for him (and that surprise was in the form of a clear STD test and now officially having been on birth control for two weeks).

He was clean.

He'd known that because he'd just had a physical and that had been part of the regular screening.

She'd gotten tested right after everything happened with Daniel, but she'd wanted to be sure, wanted to know for certain before they ditched the condoms.

Plus, now she had insurance and a doctor through her new job (another tie cut between her and Daniel, thank God), so she might as well use them.

So her surprise for him was her.

Packaged in lace.

And it was also her heart.

Packaged in...*her.*

Grinning—which made it very difficult to slick on one more layer of lipstick—she finished getting ready and was just spritzing herself with one squirt of perfume when the doorbell rang.

Heart suddenly in her throat, she held her eyes in the mirror. "You love him. It will all be okay."

She knew that he wouldn't turn away the gift of her.

She knew it because he loved her, too.

She saw it in his eyes when he looked at her. She saw it in the gentle way he touched her. She saw it in the way he was with her boys and how he'd come to her for help and...

She saw it now as she opened the front door to reveal him standing on the porch, eyes blazing with love—and heat—as he looked her up and down. His gaze was a heated touch, staring at her toes, drifting up her shins, her thighs, the hem of her dress dancing several inches above her knees. It was as though he was stroking his fingers up between her legs, teasing them over the lace that covered her most intimate parts. Then his gaze was moving again, sliding over her middle, pausing for long enough on her breasts that her nipples ached for his touch, that the dampness of her desire soaked through that lace. Up further, along her throat, over her face, her hair, and finally dipping to meet her eyes.

One corner of his mouth tipped up. "Nice dress, sweetpea."

"Nice suit," she whispered back. "Though it's kind of fancy for a movie."

He lifted a hand, dragged a thumb lightly over her bottom lip then turned that digit toward his face, as though surprised that her lipstick didn't so much as budge. But she'd put the good stuff on tonight, so not a trace of red marked his thumb.

"You can't even kiss it off," she murmured.

His eyes slid from his thumb back to hers. "No?"

She shook her head. "Nope." A beat, resisting the urge to clamp her teeth into her bottom lip. "Wanna try?"

The question had barely crossed her lips before his mouth was on hers. The air left her lungs in a rush when she found herself pinned between the door and Ben's big, hard body. Then his mouth was on hers and she wasn't thinking about lace or her lipstick.

She was *feeling*.

His mouth on hers, his lips parting, his tongue stroking, his hands holding her close.

Love and heat, desire and need. Pleasure and joy and—

He tore his mouth from hers, leaving them both breathing heavy. "Look at that." He rubbed his thumb over her bottom lip. "Still bright, fuckable red."

"We could...you know"—she glanced over her shoulder—"go and give it our best effort." Yearning was tearing its way through her body, leaving her exhales shaky, her thighs trembling, her pussy wet, her breasts aching for his touch. But he didn't take the invitation, didn't push her further inside, forget dinner and take her to her bedroom so they could test the efficacy of that new doorknob.

Instead, he reached for her coat hanging on the rack by the door, snagged her purse from the small table in the hall.

The former he slipped around her.

The latter, he gripped in one big hand, using the other to draw her outside, keeping her close and steady, showing her that desire tempered with love.

He reached into his pocket, locked up, still making sure she was steady.

Which parted the haze of desire clouding her mind.

Because he was caring for her. Watching out for her. *Loving* her.

She looked up at him, at the gorgeous kind face who'd helped her rescue herself, who'd helped her believe in herself, who'd helped her—

"I love you."

It was a total blurt.

Almost a shout.

And considering that their faces were all of a couple of inches apart, she basically just declared her love for this man by screaming at him.

Once, she might have shut down at that, would have spent long minutes considering how to melt into the floor and die a thousand deaths.

Today, having this man, knowing *herself*, she stepped closer to him—which basically meant that she shifted in his hold, pressing her front to his, reaching up and cupping his cheeks in her palms. "I love you, honey," she said—not shouted. "I need you to know."

His eyes had gone wide.

They were still warm, still on hers, but there was surprise in their depths and then...

The slightest bit of irritation.

That blip of annoyance cascaded over her like an arctic water-fall, chilling her straight down to the bone.

Her stomach clenched tight.

Her hands dropped away from his face.

Had she...

Had she completely misjudged this man?

THIRTY-FOUR

BEN

He saw the moment she'd begun to doubt herself, the moment she'd begun to retreat.

And that withdrawal, the slice of hurt she had slipping into her expression, finally cut through his surprise.

"You had to do it, didn't you?"

She started to pull away, but he banded an arm around her waist, drew her flush against him again.

"You just had to," he said again, smoothing his knuckles over her cheek.

Her chin came up, and he saw the retort form on her lips.

Kissing her to stop it from escaping, to taste that bit of fire he loved to see, he held her close until she melted.

Only then did he break the kiss, did he pull back enough to tell her, "I'm teasing, sweetpea."

Her brows dragged together.

"I had an entire evening planned, honey." He gently smoothed away her frown. "I had all these plans to tell you that I love you, and then you just went and jumped the gun, didn't you?" His lips were tipping up, wanting to make sure she was in on the joke.

And she was.

Because the retreat halted, the coolness disappeared. That warmth that was his favorite thing on the planet reappeared.

"You've got a woman who knows what she wants, what she's feeling, who she is." A press of her lips to his. "And I love you and I love to make you smile and feel good and make sure you know that my love is real." Arms drifting up, slinging around his neck. "Which means that you're going to have to deal with being one-upped on a regular basis."

"Don't you know to not get competitive with a hockey player?" he teased.

"Don't *you* know to not get competitive with a mom who settles disagreements with UNO?" she teased back.

Laughter in his chest, his heart, his soul.

"I love you," he said, dropping his forehead to hers. "You know that, right?"

"I know it."

"Good," he told her. "Now we're going to pretend that we didn't just say what we just said because we're going out to dinner at a fancy restaurant, and then you're getting a special dessert with those words written on the plate...and that was a pain in the ass to arrange, so you're going to have to pretend to be surprised."

Her eyes widened, and then he had *her* laughter in his soul.

And it was fucking perfect.

———

Josh dropped the kids off the next morning, sans the side of naked bedside time and black eyes.

It was Sunday.

He had to be at the Gold Mine in a couple of hours.

But Jordyn had been pulled into an after-hours call for her new job (some crisis for a time zone on the opposite side of the world, where it was actually Monday and a workday already), so he and the boys had been shepherded outside.

Fine with him.

It was a beautiful day and he liked being with them, being in nature, even if that nature was just the grass and trees and flowers of a large back yard.

Now, though, the boys had been tired out from kicking a soccer ball around—Sammy nearly at full strength, despite his unwieldy cast. Soon that would be off his arm altogether and Ben knew that Sammy would be outpacing him with very little effort. But with the cast weighing him down, he'd eventually caved and was lying next to Ben and Marcus on the grass, who were staring up at the partly-cloudy sky, finding increasingly ridiculous shapes in the ever-shifting clouds.

"That looks like a half-robot, half-elephant," Marcus said, barely able to get the words out before he burst out laughing.

His head was on Ben's stomach, legs sprawled out in front of him, Sammy mirroring his position on the opposite side.

"Yeah!" Sammy said, jabbing a finger in the direction of the robot elephant. "Look, there's his robot arms."

"And his trunk," Marcus said, pointing. "Oh, Sammy. Do you see that one? It looks like an alligator."

"Just a plain old alligator?" he asked.

"With a jet pack!" Sammy added.

"You're right. Look, Ben. There are the flames"—Marcus pointed to some misshapen cloud that appeared to be missing all signs of jet packs and flames, at least according to his adult brain —"and there's the straps."

"Yeah!" Sammy jumped up, excitement making him wriggle as always.

And Ben was...fuck, he loved these boys already.

They were great and it just boggled his mind that their father was missing out on this, on these boys and their sharp minds, on these boys and the kindness and warmth they spread, even their bickering and subsequent UNO argument settling were lovable.

That Daniel didn't see it that way—

Well, he would never understand it, so continuing to ponder that question was a waste of time and energy.

The latter, he wasn't going to waste any more of, not when he'd rather save it for Marcus and Sammy. The former, he didn't have enough of, so no more squandering of it.

He needed to leave in—he lifted his hand, checked the time on his smart watch—twenty minutes to head to the rink.

His pregame routine wasn't crazy, not like some of the guys', but he needed enough time to warm up properly, legs, body, hands, enough time to get his head in the game. And enough time to get all of his gear on, though he'd done that so often over the years that he could breeze right through that part in mere minutes if he had to.

A third of an hour left to enjoy these boys, this moment.

So he just carefully set his arm down and listened to them chatter. Then listened to them fall silent, all of their thoughts on the clouds moving peacefully overhead.

Or so he thought.

Because Marcus was, apparently, thinking of different things.

"Ben?" he asked.

"Yeah, bud?"

"Are you our new dad?"

His mouth dropped open. "Uh..."

Sammy sat up, his cast digging into Ben's belly, stealing whatever remained of his breath. Marcus did the same, albeit without the cast-digging.

And then there were two boys with Jordyn's eyes sitting next to him and waiting for him to answer what would probably be one of the most important questions ever asked of him.

Because he wanted to be their dad.

He knew that he would be a fuck of a lot better father than their biological one was.

He'd had plenty of experience with bad examples, so he knew he wouldn't fuck it up.

But, the truth was, they already had a father.

Sammy's face started to fall, and he realized he was still lying there like a lump.

Quickly, he sat up, eyes going to Marcus then to Sammy. "Is that something you guys would want?"

The boys exchanged a look and then Sammy nodded. Energetically. "Yeah."

Marcus gave him more detail. "We haven't really had a dad. It's always been Mom."

Such basic words, but already Ben could see how much that truth was hurting Marcus and Sammy. God, Daniel was such a fucker. "I didn't really have a dad growing up either," he told them.

"Was he always working like our dad?" Sammy asked.

"No," Ben said. "He...um...couldn't be what we needed, so he left. And then it was just me and my sister and my mom."

Marcus's eyes went wide. "You have a sister?"

"Yeah," he said. "Maddy's younger than me."

"Can we meet her?" Sammy asked.

"Soon, hopefully."

"And you'll be our new dad now?" Sammy was practically vibrating with excitement. "Because you like our mom and that means you like us too and—"

Marcus elbowed him. "Be cool."

"Hey!" Sammy snapped. "I *am* cool."

"You're both cool," Ben intervened, "and I do like your mom. A lot. Almost as much as I like you guys. But—" Marcus's face flashed with such hurt that it caused actual, visceral pain in Ben's heart. "But," he said again. "You already have a dad, so I can't be that. Not right at this moment."

The boys deflated and he gave them the truth, even though it was probably too old for them, even though they probably wouldn't understand all of it. But—for him—he needed them to have it, needed to start off like this. Because he planned on being in their lives forever.

And he wasn't going to fuck that up.

"It's too soon for you guys to make that choice and probably too soon for your mom, too. But I can be Ben. I can be *your* Ben, your mom's Ben, and maybe someday when you're ready for it and your mom is ready for it, I can be your dad in some way." He held their eyes. "In a way that you guys get to decide because anyone would be really lucky to be your dad, most especially me."

They were silent.

"Is that okay with you guys?"

Still silent.

But then Marcus said, "I still want you to be our new dad."

"Me too," Sammy added.

"Okay, bud. But for now, I'll be your Ben?"

The boys considered that for long enough that Ben began to sweat.

"Can we still go to Gold games?" Marcus asked. "And you'll still watch me play soccer?"

He ruffled Marcus's hair. "Of course."

"And me?" Sammy asked. "When I can play?"

"Absolutely."

The boys looked at each other again for a long time, long enough that sweat began to drip down his back.

Then Marcus nodded, seemingly having finished the nonverbal conversation with Sammy. "And you'll still take us all to the Dairy?"

He grinned.

These boys had their priorities straight.

"Definitely."

Then he had two tight hugs around his middle, two sets of arms squeezing him so hard that he could barely breathe.

The Dairy worked miracles.

Then again—he thought back to that first magical night with their mom there—he already knew that.

THIRTY-FIVE

"Do you think that our Ben will like our new Lego set?" Sammy asked, shaking the car with his typical excitement as they pulled up to the curb in front of Ben's place.

Our Ben.

Her heart squeezed tight every time she heard the boys call him that.

It had been a week since he'd come into the office, needing to head out to the rink, but needing to discuss the fact that the boys had asked him to be their new dad.

That had...hurt.

Ben had known, because of course he knew.

But he'd taken her in his arms and explained what he'd told them—which wasn't what she would have told them, full disclosure, but she tended to want to protect them from the truth about what had happened with Daniel.

And she'd known he'd made the right call for himself, for the relationship he was building with her boys.

They were growing to love each other.

And who better to show them what a real man, a real father, could be like than someone whose dad hadn't been there for him, too? Ben would show them that real relationships took work, would show them that a real father stuck around and earned respect and loyalty, that a real father loved even without fancy titles and despite biology.

So yeah, not what she would have told them.

But, she got it.

And the boys got it.

And she'd spent the last week watching them strengthen the bond between them.

And *Our Ben* was just the beginning of it.

Today, Sammy had gotten his cast off. His arm was weak and a little sore, but he'd still been up to celebrate at the Lego Store.

And she'd gone a little crazy, letting the boys get one small set each and then a big one with lots of pieces to build with Ben.

Because the Falcon was done (and taking up an obscene amount of space—no pun intended—on the dining room table at her place), so clearly they needed something else to build together. Or, at least, that was the argument that had won her over.

She liked that they'd already started forming ties, that they had things they did together.

Just the boys.

They'd been sorely lacking on that, visits to and from Uncle Josh's place not nearly enough.

So, she was feeding that connection.

With Legos that would probably end up on the carpet for her to step on, just based on painful past experience.

She put the van into park, turned off the ignition, and was just getting out when Ben came out the front door. Which, of course, sent the boys into a tizzy, a flurry of seat belts unbuckling and bags being grabbed.

They flew up the walk, collided so hard with Ben that they sent their big, strong Ben back a pace.

But then he scooped them up, one under each arm.

"Where'd your cast go, Sammy Sams?" he joked.

"The doctor cut it off with a *big* saw!" Sammy cried, extending his arms—and also the distinctive yellow bag dangling from his wrist—forward like he was a flying superhero. "And now I'm *free!*"

"Make us fly, Ben!" Marcus cried, extending his arms—and bag—too.

Jordyn went to the trunk, pulled out the larger yellow bag, just as Ben was setting the boys on the porch. "Fly inside, little superheroes," he said. "I'm gonna help your mama."

Then he was next to her, his spice in her nose, his body close.

"What's this?" he asked, smirking as he snagged the bag from her hand.

"A surprise for Our Ben."

His eyes softened and he peeked inside. "Spoiling me?"

She smoothed her hand over his jaw, the bristles there tickling her skin. "Nothing's too good for my boys."

A brush of his lips to hers. "Funny, I was going to say the same about my boys *and* girl."

Lifting on tiptoe, she took one more kiss. "I missed you."

Knuckles on her cheek. "Missed you too, sweetpea." Then his arm was around her waist and he was leading her toward the house. "All go good with Sammy's appointment?"

She loved him.

God, she was such a sap, but she loved this man so much.

Nodding, she gave him the rundown. "How was the flight?"

A shrug, his lips parting, but anything he might have told her about it was cut off by the sound of a car pulling into the driveway.

He frowned, started to turn, and then went ramrod stiff. "Fuck," he muttered.

"What?" she asked as the engine turned off, the driver's door pushed open.

"My mom."

Jordyn sucked in a breath, but though Ben started to drop her arm—and they'd talk about *that,* about his trying to put distance between them, later—she caught it, kept her side to his. "I'm here," she whispered.

The tension didn't completely leave his frame, but he relaxed marginally, and his fingers wrapped back around her waist.

"Hey, honey," his mom called, halfway out of the door. "I—"

But then she froze, as though just realizing that Jordyn was there.

"Mom," Ben said in greeting, drawing them both down the walk. "This is Jordyn. My girlfriend."

His mother somehow went even more still. "Your girlfriend?"

There was something in that question that prickled across Jordyn's skin, but then again, based on everything that Ben had told her, she figured she was already predisposed to not like the woman who'd hefted so much upon his shoulders. Now, she focused on being polite.

She loved this man.

She'd have to interact with his mother, no matter how much she disliked her.

Not the best way to start off a relationship, but...

It was the truth, and if she'd learned anything over the last months, it was that she needed to live her truth.

"Yeah, Mom. My girlfriend."

The affirmation didn't unstick his mom, or not in the way that Jordyn expected anyway.

Ben's mom spun away from them, turned to her trunk, and lifted the hatch.

Ben's fingers flexed and Jordyn didn't know if it was because his mom had turned away or because his mom's response to the fact that Ben had a girlfriend was turning away —no *Nice to meet yous,* no fluff, no handshakes or hugs or anything that resembled excitement over the fact that Ben had found someone.

Yeah.

She was *not* a fan of this woman.

But Ben's mom was pulling out bags, so politeness took over. "Here," she said, hurrying over. "Let me help you."

Ben's mom jerked away from Jordyn, as though Jor were polluting her space.

And no joke, that stung a little, but mostly, it pissed her off.

So she decided to adopt blitheness, reaching into the trunk, snagging the bags. "I'm sure Ben appreciates you stopping by. Should I grab all these?"

"Ben!"

Not his mother.

Her boys.

They'd run out onto the porch.

"Can we build our Legos?"

That unstuck Ben finally. His face softened and she knew that his mom saw it because she sucked in a breath and when Jordyn glanced up at her, the stark pain on her face, the longing...it was clear to anyone who looked.

Okay, maybe she hated this woman slightly less than she'd anticipated.

"Come help us with these bags," she called, making Ben's mom jump. "Then you can take your Legos into the living room and build your sets."

Legos were a good motivator, so she didn't have any complaints on her hands.

They just ran over, grabbed a couple of bags.

But the problems started when Marcus saw that one of the bags had junk food. "Is this for your Cheat Day, Ben?"

"No, bud," he said quietly.

Marcus frowned, but when he glanced up at her, she shook her head slightly and he didn't ask anything else.

Sammy, though, didn't get the hint. "But you're not supposed to eat junk food normally."

"I know."

Sammy tugged on Ben's mom's hand. "Why did you bring food Our Ben can't eat?"

"Sammy," Jordyn interjected, even though that was the question of the hour. "Just take the bag in, okay? I know you want to build your Legos."

Thankfully, Sammy took the bag without further argument.

And Marcus trailed him into the house.

"I'll just—" She reached for the bags—

"That was rude of him."

A quiet statement, but one that prickled down Jordyn's spine like steel wool and ate away any sympathy that she'd conjured up.

"Mom!" Ben snapped.

His mom shrugged, glanced back to the bags, started angrily yanking them out.

"Probably, not the most polite question for my *six*-year-old" —emphasis on Sammy's age, only two years younger than Ben had been when the weight of his family had fallen onto his shoulders—"but he *is* six, and considering the question was the same one I was thinking..." She trailed off, let that sit in the air between them, and turned to Ben. "Do you want me to come back to you after I drop off the bags of food you won't eat?"

A brush of his knuckles to her cheek. "I always want you to come back." A gentle smile. "But I need to talk to my mom." His gaze drifted up, over Jordyn's shoulder to where his mom was standing.

"Alone."

THIRTY-SIX

"*That's* your girlfriend?" his mom sneered, and the last semblance of his control snapped.

Still, he resisted the urge to throttle her.

She had no clue. *No* clue. She'd never fucking had.

"And with two rude kids?" she asked, snatching the handle of the bag and yanking it forward in a jerky, angry movement. "Questioning *me*," she muttered, her eyes and mind clearly not on him any longer—something he knew from experience rather than a particular change in behavior or tone. "I know my son better than anyone—"

"Are you fucking serious?"

Normally, he tuned her out when she began grumbling to herself, bemoaning the fact that the whole world was against her, but she was talking about Marcus and Sammy. She was talking about the boys.

His boys.

Who'd lain with him on the grass and made up fake animals out of the clouds, who'd rested their heads on his belly and asked him serious questions. Who'd built Legos with him and treaded softly when he'd been upset after Maddy, knowing instinctively that he'd needed it. Who were so bright, so kind, so fucking *wonderful* that no one in their right mind would think they were rude.

Except his mother.

But she wasn't in her right mind, hadn't been for years.

He loved her, God help him, but he did. He could remember the good times from before his dad had left, remember how she'd made every day fun and special. She'd been a good mom, but she hadn't been *that* good mom, not for a long, long time.

And he'd finally found someone, multiple someones, who made him happy.

He wasn't going to jeopardize that, not even in the memory of the mom he loved.

"Mom," he said when she didn't answer him and instead just continued grabbing bags, huffing all the while. *"Mom."* He snagged her arm, halting her bag retrieval. "Stop," he said when she tried to shake him off and reach for the bags again. *"Just stop."*

Something in his tone finally seemed to get through to her because she did pause her efforts.

"Look at me."

Her gaze stayed firmly on the ground.

"Look at me."

Her eyes finally shot to his, and he caught a glimpse of something that finally clued him in as to how to handle this.

"You fucked up," he told her.

She flinched.

Yeah, it wasn't the kindest thing to say, to handle her, but he'd spent the last two decades handling her with kid gloves. He was done.

He needed her to see.

He needed her to understand.

So he pressed on.

"You fucked up when Dad left," he said. "There's no two ways around it. You should have been there for Maddy and me, not functioning at so low of a level that I'm the only parental figure Maddy knows. Knew." He shrugged. "Then you fucked up again by marrying Bill and not seeing him for what he was, not having the type of relationship with Maddy that you should have, so that she could have trusted you enough to go to when Bill hurt her."

More flinches.

Tears in her eyes.

"I know you blame me. I know Maddy blames me. But"—he sucked in a breath, released it slowly—"it was you who should have been there for me. *You* should have been there for *me* and her. *You* fucked up, and I've carried the guilt of wishing I could have been there, wishing I'd known, wishing I'd said fuck all to my future and continued living my life for yours for too long."

"Maddy—"

"I saw Maddy," he said. "We had a conversation very similar to this one. And you know what her response was?"

His mom shook her head.

"She fucking thought about what *I* was feeling for a change. She reflected and thought about where the blame was and what she wanted and she's going to try, Mom." He shook his head. "Not because I'm paying for the rehab and forcing her to go. But because she wants it and wants to go it alone."

"She can't do it by herself."

"No," he agreed. "She's going to need support from us. Of course, she is. But she's going to need it on her terms, not you flitting in and offering breadcrumbs when you get a whim to."

"I—"

"You suck as a mom."

Now her flinch was more of a stagger, and maybe he should feel guilty, maybe this would send her off the rails again.

But what did he have to lose by giving her the long-overdue truth?

Nothing.

Because he couldn't continue going on as he was.

So, he gave her the bald facts and didn't spare her feelings.

"That woman inside. The woman I *love* in a way I never thought possible didn't leave her kids when her husband cheated on her with her best friend." His mom's eyes widened and she staggered back another step. "She didn't shut down or make them shoulder the responsibility to pick up the pieces, not like I had to do. Instead, she gathered her strength and packed them up and started their lives over. She found a way to give them the people they need, and I'm one of those people." He thumped a fist to his chest. "And I'm not fucking that up because those boys are innocent and kind and wonderful and *they*"—he flung out a hand toward the house—"*they* know that I can't eat this shit. It only took me once mentioning it and they got on board to understand and support me in that. And months is all I've known them. Just *months* and they—all three of them own my fucking heart—know what I can eat. But my mom, my *mom* who I've told a dozen times over the last couple of years I've been on this plan, doesn't know or doesn't care or—"

"Ben."

He sucked in a breath, released it.

"You don't care," he said. "And I don't know how you went from the mom I had for eight years to the one I've had for the last two decades, but I'm done walking on eggshells. I'm done trying to cater to you."

"Ben, I love you."

"I know." A beat. "But you have a shit way of showing it. So, you either forgive me for living my life, stop trying to undermine the choices I've made, and find a way to be the mom I loved again, or I'm done. Done," he repeated when her eyes sparked with anger. "Because I will not let you fuck up the best thing I've ever had. They"—another toss of his hand toward the house—"don't deserve it, and I'm finally understanding that I don't deserve it either."

Silence.

The sparks in her eyes gone.

Her face stark in its pain and grief.

But he wasn't going to give in, wasn't going to yield. Not in this. Not now. It was too important. *They* were too important.

His happiness was too important.

"I want you in my life," he said softly. "I miss that mom I loved. I miss her so f-fucking much." He blinked back tears, throat suddenly tight. "But if you bring this attitude again to the people who've respected my love, who've held it close and protected it like the precious gift it is, then we're done."

Surprised eyes came to his.

"No more, Mom," he said.

A tear dripped down her cheek. Then another.

But he didn't let it soften his resolve.

Instead, he took the rest of the bags and closed the trunk. "You walk over the threshold of my house and you come in as the mom I loved." He turned back, waited until she met his eyes. "Or you don't come in at all."

He spun for the house.

"Wh-what if I don't know how?"

Glancing over his shoulder, he told her the truth. "You're smart. You'll figure it out." A beat, his eyes holding hers, so he saw when his next words had her eyes tearing up again.

"This is your chance to do it differently."

THIRTY-SEVEN

Ben came in as the boys were just settling into their Legos, his face stark, and his arm full of bags.

He'd left the front door open behind him, but she didn't comment on that particular statement.

Instead, she just moved toward him, took some of the bags from his hands, and set her load on the counter. Then she waited for him to set his burden down.

Then finally, she was able to take him in her arms, to hold him tight.

He didn't say anything and neither did she.

Because sometimes words weren't needed.

Eventually, he sighed, kissed the side of her neck and straightened, brushing his knuckles over her cheek.

"Hey," he said.

"Hey," she murmured back. "I've got dinner sorted." She nodded toward the ingredients she'd pulled out of the fridge (a fridge that he'd begun to actually stock—instead of the desert wasteland that had previously occupied the same space —since she and the boys had been eating with him here once or twice a week). "Some of the stuff you can eat"—another nod, this time to the small pile of food she'd extracted from the bags that actually went with the meal plan he was on—"others the boys will definitely devour"—some of the junk food would go down like a house on fire —"but some they won't"—the last pile, which was, unfortunately, also the largest—"so I wasn't sure what you normally do with it."

"Throw it in the trash."

She wasn't sure if that was a reference to what he normally did with it, or a directive in that moment.

She also didn't get her answer.

Because there was a sharp inhale behind Ben, and they both turned to see his mother standing there.

Jordyn braced.

But instead of a retort, as she'd expected, Ben's mom glanced at her feet for a long moment.

Then her shoulders rose and fell as though she'd taken a long, long inhale and then let it out, just as slowly. She looked up, closed the door, and then Jordyn watched as she seemed to brace herself up from the inside out.

A glimmer of respect, but just the barest one.

This woman had hurt her man and that wasn't an easy thing for Jordyn to abide by.

She kept an arm around Ben, shifting so it was around his waist, her body close.

Then held her breath as the other woman approached.

But all Ben's mother did was extend her hand and say, "I'm Lydia."

"Jordyn," she said, shaking Lydia's hand.

"I—" Lydia faltered then lifted her chin slightly, resolve entering her expression. "I apologize for what I said about your boys. They were right. I should have known better."

Surprise flowing through her. "Thank you for apologizing. I'm so—"

Ben squeezed her to him, cutting off her apology, and giving her a pointed look. Okay then, no trying to smooth things over.

That would have to come from his mom.

Message received.

"Take it to the food bank."

It was a burst of words, the intonation off.

But then Lydia cleared her throat. "I'll um...pack it up and take it to the food bank. It's good food," she said. "Just"—she swallowed hard—"not for my boy."

Silence and she was glad the boys were in the other room, because, God, the tension in this room was making Jordyn's skin prickle. "I think that's a good idea," she said softly.

Lydia nodded.

Ben was silent, tense, and seemingly ready to smack his mom back in line for the smallest prevarication.

This was going to be a long dinner.

"Do you want to pack up the food?" Jordyn asked when Lydia and Ben just stood there staring at each other. "I'll help you carry it out when you're done."

A startled look on Lydia's face. "Okay." She blinked. "That would be great, thanks."

Ben squeezed her again, but it was gentle.

A thanks.

She started to turn to him, to tell him thanks weren't necessary, but then footsteps pounded down the hall and Sammy spun around the corner, his Lego car in his hand. "Look, Ben!"

And then Ben was being Ben.

And that was wonderful.

He bent in front of Sammy, checked out every single detail—from the working doors to the cool details on the dashboard to the trunk that actually opened and closed. Then he did the same when Marcus brought in his scene for inspection.

Lydia slowly turned away from the scene, heading to the counter, packing the food into the bags.

Jordyn moved over to her, sorting through the rest of the

items Ben had brought in. "It still does my heart in to see him with my boys," she murmured, passing over a couple of the soon-to-be donated items. "He's really good with them."

Lydia went still, eyes glassy with tears.

Then she blinked and they were gone. "That doesn't surprise me in the least. He's a good man." Her voice dropped. "Not that I had anything to do with that."

Not said like she was playing the martyr.

But instead it was reflective, contemplative, as though whatever he'd said outside had impacted her a lot.

"You can change that starting today," she said, softening that with a smile. "And that's me speaking from experience."

Lydia stilled.

Then she reached out and squeezed Jordyn's hand. "Thank you," she murmured. "Just...thank you for loving my boy the way he deserves."

She patted Lydia's hand, respecting the statement, but not entirely won over. That would take time.

Hopefully, Lydia would rise to the occasion.

"Now's your chance to do the same," she told Ben's mom.

To her credit, Lydia didn't throw attitude back at Jordyn.

She just nodded and said, "I know."

And Jordyn thought that maybe there was hope for her yet.

———

The next two weeks passed peacefully, and though Lydia was a small presence in their lives (she'd come over to Ben's once and then had accepted Jordyn's dinner invitation two nights before), Jordyn was hopeful that Lydia might have actually turned over a new leaf.

That night, she actually brought cookies that were both delicious and abided by Ben's meal plan.

Plus, she'd played Legos with the boys for a solid hour—so they were already halfway in love with her.

Obviously, she was joking, but the truth was it both seemed like Lydia was trying and her boys were always good at making people feel welcome, especially those who played Legos with them.

And while there hadn't been any word from Maddy, they'd decided that no news was good news at this point.

So, Ben's personal life was a much lighter burden.

Her life was on track—her job was awesome, the boys had made friends, Sammy had even been able to join a soccer team though the season was halfway over.

And she'd had her attorney send Daniel divorce papers with her having sole custody.

She wanted that chapter of her life closed, and she wanted it to be official.

Not taking any chances with her boys...who were currently running down the grassy hill in front of school, tearing toward her like tiny wrecking balls.

She braced herself, and *still,* the impact nearly took her down.

But this was, no joke, the best part of her day.

Their big smiles and tight hugs. The rapid recitation of who'd played with who and who'd sat with who and what they did in science or music.

All the little details that colored their lives.

She needed to know every single one of them.

The chatter continued all the way to the car and the entire drive home. But she didn't mind, not when each of them was taking turns nicely, these interactions no longer marred by the angry resentment and competition that had taken over after the initial separation.

Now they were happy.

Now that happy showed in every aspect of their life.

And she was so thankful for them, that they were back to themselves.

Not that they were perfect. They still fought enough that the UNO deck got a regular workout.

But the sharp edges had been filed off.

The vein of hurt had been filled in.

They were back to being her boys.

And that, along with their chatter, had brought a smile to her face as she pulled into the driveway of her house (*her*, yup! See how much progress she'd made).

It kept the smile in place as she parked and the boys started to unload all their water bottles and backpacks and jackets and various art projects and worksheets.

It kept the smile in place until she turned for the porch—

And saw Daniel standing there.

THIRTY-EIGHT

They'd just arrived at the hotel.

Their game wasn't until tomorrow, but they had a light practice in the morning, and they always flew out early to accommodate any delays that might crop up.

But tonight, he was on East Coast time. The boys were just getting out of school and he was mentally tallying how long it would take for them to get home. Though, they had soccer practice today, so he might have to catch them later tonight.

Because he'd seen or talked to them (and even talking meant seeing because they video chatted when he was on the road) every single day since Maddy had gone back to rehab.

They were part of him.

Luckily, he was used to staying up late, so he knew he'd catch them at some point that day.

Now, though, he needed food, and he needed to get his shit up to his room, though not necessarily in that order.

He got his key from Nicole—one of the teams' latest batch of interns, though it looked like she might stick around when her internship ended—and dropped off his luggage, connecting with Axel, Rome, and Will on the way down.

They all decided they were too lazy to go out anywhere and just ended up at the hotel restaurant, sitting around a large round table, waters in front of them, shooting the shit about everything and nothing.

Or at least, he, Axel, and Rome were shooting the shit.

Will was...staring at Lily like she was the key to the universe... or maybe the key to *his* universe.

She sat at the bar, a stack of papers in front of her, a laptop open, hair falling in front of her face.

Beautiful, tiny, and pixie-like...and totally ignoring the group of them—or more specifically, ignoring Will (or pretending to because Ben didn't miss how she wasn't turning the pages in the files or actually typing anything on her laptop, didn't miss how she kept looking at Will out of the corner of her eye).

But she was markedly good at making it so Will didn't pick up on that.

Sneaky.

Ben didn't know what was going on between them, but clearly something was up, and he was giving himself permission to have all the nosy Brit vibes, albeit his way.

Watching.

Making plenty of mental notes.

Pouncing when appropriate.

Though, he supposed, that was Brit and her nosy matchmakingness to a T.

Smothering a grin, he sipped from his water—today was a non-Cheat Day—and then focused on the conversation at hand.

"And then she just pulled out her shotgun on me and went full John Wayne."

Rome's eyes were wide. "And you were naked?"

Axel nodded. "And handcuffed to her porch."

Okay, Ben had missed a lot in that conversation.

"And you like her, Balls?" Ben asked, using the nickname Axel had earned when he'd first been brought up from the Rush, the Gold's AHL team. "Like her enough to tolerate being handcuffed naked to her porch?"

"I like her." Axel shrugged. "More than I should, and I'm definitely fine with naked handcuffing. Though, next time I can do without the splinters in my ass." His smile was nothing short of cat-ate-the-canary. "Still worth it."

Ben smirked. "Better you than me, man."

Will turned his attention back to Lily, and this time Rome and Axel both noticed. The three of them exchanged raised brows, but Will was too focused on Lily to notice their amusement—or at least for Ben's part, he was too busy to notice Ben's nosy gossip-mindedness.

"What's up with that?" Rome said softly.

Ben shrugged.

Axel hissed back. "Don't look at me. I'm the new guy."

Lily and Will.

The girl he didn't want to talk about.

That much was clear.

The rest of it, though? Why they couldn't actually look at each other?

Ben didn't know.

But he couldn't wait to figure it out.

———

He texted Jordyn when he got back up to his room, but as he'd expected, there was no response.

Not worried, he showered, dressed, and spent some time stretching.

With the season picking up, he needed to make sure that he wasn't losing any of his flexibility. Soreness, tight muscles, they could fuck with the game, could fuck with his *head*.

Could make him tentative, not wanting to make a particular movement because it would hurt, even if that hesitation wasn't conscious, even if it were buried beneath the surface and affected him most when he was relying on instinct.

So, he did his Mandy-recommended routine of stretches.

He put on his pajamas—okay, he took off his shirt, tugged on a pair of loose basketball shorts, and called that good.

Then he texted Jordyn again.

It was almost bedtime. Normally, he would have already spoken with her—or at the very least, she would have texted back.

But it was a busy time of year, and she was on her own with two boys who were nonstop.

He...was sitting in a hotel room, stretching and twiddling his thumbs, and thinking about his freaking pajamas.

No surprise, time was passing at a snail's pace.

Determined to ignore the prickling in the back of his brain, to not worry over the fact that she hadn't contacted him yet, he put on a game. It was for the team they'd be playing in three days' time, so it was good for him to watch, to study and look for any breakdowns that he could exploit. Then he did some of his prep for the next day, looking through the tape that Jess and Dani had prepared for him, both of his opponent and of his own game play during the last few matches against them. It was an invaluable resource for him.

But his mind wasn't in it that evening.

Not a hundred percent anyway.

Because even though he *knew* that Jordyn was just busy and probably busying herself through soccer and dinner and home-work and bath time and just hadn't had time to text back, he couldn't go to sleep.

So, he gave in to the prickle, that worry, and he called her.

But she didn't pick up.

And she didn't pick up when he called an hour later.

Nor did she reply to any of the texts—not to the ones earlier in the evening, nor to the ones he sent in between or after those phone calls.

"Fuck," he whispered as he typed out an email.

But even *that* went unanswered.

And as the evening grew later and more calls rang clean through to Jordyn's voicemail, more texts were left on read, Ben's mind began working in overtime.

And none of his thoughts were good.

THIRTY-NINE

"What the hell are you doing here?" she hissed as Daniel came close.

He ignored her—but then again, he was really good at that—and leaned close, kissing her on the cheek.

Then he gave each of the boys a hug.

"Good to see you," he told them, more semi-friendly acquaintance than father, their arms wrapping dutifully around his waist, their expressions bland, their eyes...well, she didn't like what was in their eyes.

But she needed to deal with this initial crisis first.

Because even though Daniel wasn't bending, wasn't squatting and getting down to the boys' level, wasn't even asking them questions, seeing what was happening with them, even though it had been months since he'd seen them, he was still there.

Worry was a taut knot in her belly.

He wasn't anything like their Ben.

And the boys seemed to know it, whether it was a conscious thought in their minds or not. What *was* obvious? The tightness in their faces, their discomfort visible. They were still polite, sure, but that was the extent of it. They were distant.

They weren't searching for something from Daniel.

Sammy wasn't extra exuberant, trying to do anything to get Daniel's attention.

Marcus wasn't hanging close, trying to tell Daniel about the books he was reading.

They had that from their Ben.

They didn't need to search it out from a man who wasn't able to give it.

That settled a few more of the jagged pieces in her soul.

"Why don't you guys go inside and get ready for practice?" she said. "Your snacks are in the fridge."

They clambered off, and she turned back to Daniel.

Searching.

For a depth of feeling that had kept her with him, searching for some indication that she'd felt *something* big and important for him, something that made sense for why she'd stay for so long.

But all her searching did was cause her to stare at him like he was a bug.

"What are you doing here?" she asked, feeling a lot calmer now that the initial shock had worn off.

"I got these."

She realized he'd set a stack of papers on the porch railing.

Now he lifted them up, handed them to her.

She peeked inside, saw they were divorce papers. *Signed* divorce papers...the ones her attorney had sent. Which was a surprise that jolted through her.

They'd expected no little amount of back and forth as they settled on terms and child support, especially considering the antipathy he'd been throwing her way for the last months.

Hell, the last years.

"Is there a reason that you're delivering them in person?"

"I had a conference in the city." His stared out at the street for a long moment. "And I needed to make sure you guys were okay."

She bit back a snort. That would be a first. He'd never seemed particularly concerned about them, even when they were together. After, even the most slender thread of concern hadn't been present, and he'd completely washed his hands of them.

"She's pregnant."

That hit hard. Jordyn couldn't lie. But she'd moved on, too. "Congrats."

He shoved his hands into his pockets, rocked back on his heels, nodded at her felicitations, and their eyes connected, held. For a moment she thought she might get some honesty, some understanding to the man she'd once loved.

But that wasn't Daniel.

That wasn't their relationship.

A fact that was made clear when he brushed his hands together and turned away from the house. "Right, then." He popped his lips. "I'm off, then."

And then he'd gotten into his car and driven away, leaving her a bit bewildered...

But with signed divorce papers in her hands.

———

"Are you—" She didn't want to bring this up, wanted to avoid it because it was easier.

But they'd been on their normal whirlwind from the moment that Daniel had left—rushing to Sammy's soccer practice, sitting on the sidelines and helping Marcus with his homework then rushing off to Marcus's team's practice while sitting with Sammy on the cooling grass doing *Sammy's* homework, then they'd had to stop at the library to pick up Marcus's latest book haul (he was out of books—*out!*—and that could not be left to stand). Now they were finally home and she needed them to clean off the grass and dirt that made it seem like they'd rolled on the ground rather than actually playing soccer—though, she supposed, they had spent a good amount of time rolling around and generally getting dirty with their buds.

All in good fun.

Still, they needed to get spic and span while she cooked dinner.

Then eat. Clean up. Text Ben back. Hopefully, he would still be up so they could talk.

Then...breathe.

Being a single mom to two busy boys and girlfriend to a professional hockey player was no freaking joke.

"Am I what?" Marcus asked, eyes glued to his book.

"Your dad showing up and leaving, I know that you have wanted—"

"We don't need him," Marcus said, tugging off his long soccer socks. She no longer had to hog-tie and wrestle him into the shower because Ben had mentioned that he always showered after hockey once. *Once!* And now Marcus was *all* about that personal hygiene. "We have our Ben now."

The knot in her belly loosened.

"I know, honey, but sometimes when people aren't able to give us what we need, it..." She sucked in a breath through her nose, released it slowly. "It hurts us sometimes."

He paused, eyes lifting, holding hers in a way that she hated.

Because they were older than they should be.

And she would never forgive Daniel for that.

"Yeah, Mom."

"So, seeing Dad come back now, it might be making you feel bad."

His fingers tightened on the edges of his book. "I used to wonder why he didn't love us."

A quiet admission that sliced right through her.

"But we have Uncle Josh and Ben and Jess and Stefan and Blane and the others." Those eyes were on hers again. "They love us. So"—a shrug—"I'm not going to waste my time on someone who can't give me what I want."

She heard Ben in those words.

But she also saw the determination on Marcus's face. Too old for his eight years. She shouldn't be having to have this conversation. He shouldn't have to think about this shit. But she couldn't deny that she thought it was the right track to allow his thoughts.

Focus on the positive.

Not continue trying to squeeze juice from an orange that was dry and pithy inside.

Her boy was smarter than her.

And she was glad for it.

"Mom?"

Blinking, she realized she'd been quiet for too long. "Yeah, baby?"

"Can I shower now? I'm hungry."

Stop torturing me with emotional talk and leave me alone so I can clean up. Oh, and cook me dinner, puh-lease.

Grinning, she kissed the top of his head, got a blade of grass in her mouth for her trouble, and then left him to his shower.

Poking her head into Sammy's bedroom and finding him playing with his Legos, she decided that she would talk to him later. Food in their bellies first, and plus, he got cranky when he was interrupted while working his building magic.

She'd just thrown some chicken breasts in the oven—doused with ranch, topped with seasoned breadcrumbs, they weren't the healthiest, but she liked to pretend they were better than fast food.

Plus, she'd added some veggies and fruit, so it was practically health food.

Still, the boys loved it, and since it was late and they'd had a busy day, they didn't fight her much on going to sleep.

But she still had dishes to do and then she wanted to sit down for a few minutes on her work laptop, just to review her schedule for the next day. Plus, she needed to find her phone. She hadn't heard from Ben and wanted to make sure he got settled into the hotel.

The knock at the door while she was mid-dish washing had her frowning.

Drying her hands on a towel as she moved from the kitchen and to the hall, she turned the door handle just as the second knock came.

She pulled the wooden panel wide, saw Daniel on the other side, and felt her jaw hit the floor.

What *the* fuck?

FORTY

BEN

Somehow, he'd fallen asleep.

It wasn't particularly restful or deep.

Which was why the moment he heard the first buzz of his phone beginning to vibrate, he shot bolt upright, saw it was Jordyn, and swiped as quickly as he could across the screen.

Quiet rustling as the video call connected and then her face was on his phone.

Relief sinking into him like a body slowly lowering into hot, hot water. For a second, it was so overwhelming that he could think of nothing but that relief, could hear nothing but the rapid pulse thrumming in his ears.

Then he finally calmed down enough to *hear* what she was saying.

"Oh my God. Oh my God. Oh my—"

That relief flew the fuck out of his system. "What, sweetpea? Are you okay? Are the boys?"

But she was just pacing back and forth, repeating that sentiment, rubbing an occasional hand over her face, shoving it through her hair.

She was at home, he saw. That pacing taking place on her back deck.

"Sweetpea."

Her eyes coming to the phone. "Sorry, I just—" She broke off, rubbing another hand over her face. "I've had a day that you would not believe."

"Are you hurt?"

"What?" She dropped her hand, blinking slowly, then finally reverted back to the Jordyn he knew and loved. "We're okay," she told him, her voice warm and soft. "*All* of us."

The worry that had gripped him over the last hours faded.

Was replaced with a touch of annoyance.

"So why didn't you call me back?" It wasn't a gentle, easy question. It was...sharp.

But before he could apologize for it, her expression went contrite. "I'm sorry, honey. I was so thrown by Daniel showing up that I've been all over the place for hours."

"*What?*"

If he'd been awake before, now he was at full alertness.

"Are you okay? The boys, are they upset or hurt or—"

"Ben, honey, *breathe*," she ordered gently. "I'm sorry. I'm really messing this all up." He watched her through the camera walk over to the chair they usually shared when they were at her house, sinking into it, the warm glow of the lights shining through the kitchen windows at her back. "We're all okay. Daniel was at the house after school. He gave me the signed divorce papers, didn't fight me on anything." Now her face when a little sad. "She's pregnant."

Ben stilled.

Shit.

He'd never hated his job more than in that moment.

Because he hadn't been there, wasn't there right now. Couldn't hold her. Couldn't stroke her skin, comfort her because her ex-husband was a fucking asshole.

"The boys"—more sad—"they barely looked at him. It was

like they were hugging some distant relative, and Daniel was...I don't fucking know." A breath. "All I *do* know is that he isn't—hasn't ever been—the father they need. And I know that you, honey..." she murmured. "You've been more of a father to them. And they know it."

His throat went tight.

"Marcus told me that they don't need him because they have you." She smiled and it was a little watery. "And Sammy," she whispered. "He built a Lego house with all four of us in it. *Four,* honey. He never did that for Daniel. It was always just him, Marcus, and me."

Fuck.

He swiped at his eyes. "Sweetpea," he rasped. "That's—"

"They love Josh and Jess and the other guys on the team. The Gold made us all a part of their family. But it's you," she whispered. "It's you who's made us complete. The boys see it. I see it. And I hope"—her lips turned up—"you know you're stuck with us."

He swiped at his eyes again, a big, clunky hockey player reduced to a puddle of emotion by the woman he loved. "You guys are the ones who are stuck with *me.*"

"I love you," she whispered.

"You're my heart."

Her mouth curved again. "I know," she told him. "Which is why it was easy to tell him to get the fuck out of my life when he came by a second time a little while ago."

He blinked. "*What?*"

"I'd just gotten the kids in bed and finished cleaning up, and I'm so sorry that I didn't see your texts and calls earlier. My phone died, and I didn't realize it until I went to call you, so I had to charge it and—" The rapid tumble of words abruptly cut off.

Probably, because he was ready to jump through the screen.

"Sorry," she said sheepishly. "I just..." She bit her lip. "He knocked on my door after the boys were in bed and wanted..."

"Jordyn," he warned when she trailed off and didn't continue.

"I don't actually know what he wanted," she whispered. "Maybe absolution. Maybe reassurance that he was going to be a good father. But how could I give him that? He's not a good father, not like you"—her eyes connected with his and they were watery—"and how could I tell him that it was okay that he fucked my best friend and now had knocked her up, that he imploded our marriage and treated me like shit?" She sighed. "I couldn't. I *couldn't*. Especially, when I know myself now, when I know what I deserve, when I know that I have someone who loves me, really loves me."

"Sweetpea," he whispered.

"I know. So I told him that and I told him that I couldn't forgive him because, fuck that, he doesn't deserve forgiveness for what he's done to his boys, to *me*, and my forgiveness would be a gift that I didn't owe him." A breath. "He didn't make an effort to know me after he'd had me, to learn me as we changed and got older and our relationship altered. He didn't make an effort to know the boys, not in my belly, not as babies, not as they got older." She shook her head. "He didn't *care* to then, and he certainly never gave me any indication that he felt *anything* except how good it felt to sink his dick into another woman, so no, I don't have to do anything but protect me and mine." Her voice steadied. "And last, I told him that he's an footnote in my life and that I won't forgive him, but that I *will* thank him because without the shit he heaped on me, I wouldn't have found you."

Every muscle in his body was locked tight.

His heart pounded. His throat was dry and all he could rasp out to all of that fucking perfection she'd unleashed on her ex was, "*Sweetpea*."

She smiled and it was a bit watery. "I know."

He finally got it together to say something better, something more important. "I am so fucking proud of you."

Her throat worked and she said again, "I know."

"What did he do then?" he asked when he was able to get actual words out without turning into a sobbing baby. She'd been there for him when he'd dealt with his mom, when everything had gone down with Maddy.

And he'd been there for her with Sammy, helping with the boys and moving.

He would have been there for her if he'd been home, *wished* he'd been there to destroy that motherfucker, but he knew—*knew* —how important it was that she was able to handle this herself. She'd questioned her strength, her capability because that asshole of an ex had picked away at her confidence.

That she was able to hand him his ass?

That was exactly what she'd needed, even if it didn't assuage his need to knock the motherfucker into the next universe.

Jordyn's smile was beatific. "He left. Just turned on his heel and walked off my porch and—" She pushed a hand through her hair. "I shut the door and I was...so freaking proud of myself that I was shaking. I could barely find my phone and the damn charger. I just had to tell you because you would get it." She sniffed. "You were the only one who would know how important it was."

He did. He got *exactly* how important it was that she'd done this.

And while he still wished he'd been there, he also knew that it was critical that she'd done it on her own.

Rebuild her confidence.

Reassign Daniel into that footnote.

"I knew you could do it."

At his statement, her eyes went gentle again, gentle and a little damp and he watched that warmth fill them, sinking into him through the video call, filling him from toes on upward, filling him to bursting when she whispered, "Sorry, I woke you up."

"Next time," he told her, waving off the apology, "keep your phone charged."

She grinned, made that promise, then added, "Can't resist taking care of me, can you?"

"Never." A beat. "Because you take care of me right back."

Epilogue

Two months later

From: Ben Roberts <ben.roberts@gold.com>
To: Jordyn Webb <jordyn@webb.com>
Subject: re: Thank you
Sweetpea,
So proud of Marcus for winning the championship game. Thanks
for sending the pictures. I hate that I missed it, but so proud
of him.
Tell Sammy good luck in his game today!
-B
P.S. You're just mean going to the Dairy without me.

From: Jordyn Webb <jordyn@webb.com>
To: Ben Roberts <ben.roberts@gold.com>
Subject: re: Thank you
Honey,
Unfortunately, they lost :(But we commiserated their loss with lots

of Lego building time, so Sammy has sufficiently recovered from his post-game sadness. His Lego house has now grown to epic proportions, so be forewarned, you're going to have to bring your master builder skills to impress him (pics included to see his awesomeness).
-J
P.S. Also, as we've previously established, cookies and cream don't go with peanut butter, so I was just doing you a favor by going to the Dairy without you.

From: Ben Roberts <ben.roberts@gold.com>
To: Jordyn Webb <jordyn@webb.com>
Subject: re: Thank you
Sweetpea,
I've got skills you haven't yet begun to see. Wink. Wink. Inserting lots of pithy emojis here.
But, seriously, I've got a plan for that house and brace yourself, it includes critters of the four-legged (and maybe a couple more of the two-legged) varieties.
Have I sent you running for the hills yet?
-B
P.S. Lies about the Dairy. Cookies and cream and peanut go perfectly together. You've admitted it before, no take-backsies now.

From: Jordyn Webb <jordyn@webb.com>
To: Ben Roberts <ben.roberts@gold.com>
Subject: re: Thank you
Honey,
Now that I've run a full circuit of the hills and back (full disclosure, I'm very out of shape)...do you maybe think that you should

spring news like that on me when—I don't know—we're actually together and not talking over email?!
-J
P.S. I want a kitten...or maybe two.

From: Ben Roberts <ben.roberts@gold.com>
To: Jordyn Webb <jordyn@webb.com>
Subject: re: Thank you
Sweetpea,
Kittens. Two. Check. We also need a dog. Or three.
-B

From: Jordyn Webb <jordyn@webb.com>
To: Ben Roberts <ben.roberts@gold.com>
Subject: re: Thank you
Honey,
Three?! You've lost your mind. Especially, if we're going to have more two-legged creatures.
-J
P.S. How many do you want? I'm not getting any younger, and I think the boys would be awesome big brothers.

From: Ben Roberts <ben.roberts@gold.com>
To: Jordyn Webb <jordyn@webb.com>
Subject: re: Thank you
Sweetpea,
Two more. Girls with your gorgeous eyes to even out the boys.
-B

P.S. Or boys. I don't care. I just want to keep you forever and make babies with you.

From: Jordyn Webb <jordyn@webb.com>
To: Ben Roberts <ben.roberts@gold.com>
Subject: re: Thank you
Honey,
And now I'm crying. I hope you're happy.
-J
P.S. I need a ring first (and for the divorce paperwork to go through). Are we crazy for talking about marriage and furbabies and actual babies this soon?

From: Ben Roberts <ben.roberts@gold.com>
To: Jordyn Webb <jordyn@webb.com>
Subject: re: Thank you
Sweetpea,
Not crazy. We both know how precious it is to find something that makes us this happy.
-B
P.S. I'll be home soon to wipe away your tears.
P.P.S. Don't forget that tomorrow is the annual Gold holiday party—a.k.a. The annual Pie Extravaganza.

From: Jordyn Webb <jordyn@webb.com>
To: Ben Roberts <ben.roberts@gold.com>
Subject: re: Thank you
Honey,
You're right. We're holding on to our happy.

-J
P.S. I still don't understand this Pie Extravaganza.

From: Ben Roberts <ben.roberts@gold.com>
To: Jordyn Webb <jordyn@webb.com>
Subject: re: Thank you
Sweetpea,
You'll see what it's like tomorrow.
-B
P.S. Cue the ominous drumroll...and empty calories.

She was still full hours after they'd poured themselves into their car.

The Pie Extravaganza was no joke.

She didn't know how she and the boys had consumed so many slices without puking them up, but she—and they—had managed.

They'd passed out in the car, post sugar crash and hours of running around with the other kids, and thankfully, Ben hadn't been so full that he hadn't been able to carry the boys into their room, so she'd just needed to crawl her way to her bedroom and then lie still for Ben's ministrations.

He'd been out of town for a week and had been full of pent-up energy, so those ministrations had equated to three orgasms and a hot, sexy hockey player spooning her from behind when she'd come back to Earth.

Now, though, she was summoning the energy to move.

The next day, Maddy and Lydia were coming over for an early Christmas celebration, and she had a million things to do to prepare the house.

For now, though, she just wanted to be in Ben's arms, to sink into sleep, to let it draw her off to oblivion.

He was home.

Every part of her felt right when he held her like this.

But she wanted to give Ben his Christmas present.

"You good, sweetpea?" he rumbled into her hair.

"Trying to summon the energy to get up."

"Why?" He squeezed her ass, drew her closer to him. "I like you here."

"Because I have a present for you," she whispered.

Suddenly, they were sitting upright.

"Presents?" he asked.

"Pre*sent*," she corrected, blinking from the sudden change in elevation and then smoothing her hand over his jaw, feeling the bristles against her skin. Then she managed to tear herself away from him and walk to the dresser, bending and tugging the envelope out of the bottom drawer. "I can feel you looking," she said.

His gaze was a warm tongue trailing over her skin, turning her hot and languid and liquid.

But she needed to focus.

"We have one more errand to make tomorrow," she murmured.

He groaned, having had it with her wanting to make their first Christmas together perfect, but it was good-natured. She knew he would go on however many errands she asked him to, with or without her.

"Here," she murmured, sitting next to him and pulling the covers up and over herself.

See? Focused.

Brows drawing together as he took in the envelope, he asked, "What's this?"

"An early Christmas present." She nudged the envelope. "Open it."

He slipped his finger under the flap, tore open the paper.

Pulled out the card she'd printed off inside.

It was a picture of the four-legged critters she'd adopted.

Yup. Critters. As in plural. As in a kitten and her best friend, a puppy, that she'd spotted on social media.

"They're ours," she whispered.

He inhaled, carefully set the photo on the nightstand, and then turned back to her, eyes damp. "Ours?"

She nodded. "The next piece of our family."

And she knew that meant just as much to him as it did to her.

He exhaled sharply then pulled her close, wrapping his arms around her and holding her tight for a long, long time.

Then he flipped them, rolling on top of her and laying a kiss on her that set her lungs burning. "Fuck, I love you."

"It's okay?" she whispered back.

Lips on hers, on her jaw, her nose, her cheek, her ear, his words soft. "It's perfect."

Then he was stripping the sheet away from her, kissing every inch of her, telling her he loved her with every caress of his mouth, his tongue, his teeth.

He paused, her thighs spread by big, warm hands, his eyes on hers. "I get to name them."

"No, I—"

He dropped his head, his tongue working a special sort of magic...

It was the magic that melted her brain and had her handing over naming privileges without further argument.

But since she'd been planning on letting Ben have the honor anyway, she considered it to be win-win.

Heh.

A woman had to know how to handle her big, sexy hockey player...

And had to know when to let him handle *her.*

Especially, if it resulted in orgasms...and a man loving every single part of her.

"Fine," he said, when he'd brought them both to and over the brink again, "you name the cat, I get the dog."

"And the boys?"

A sigh.

"They get the cat...and the dog," he grumbled.

His love for all of them shining through.

Her lips curved, and then she spent the rest of the night, even despite her full belly, letting her love for *him* shine all the way through.

Spoiler alert: it resulted in orgasms.

For him.

For her.

For *them.*

And love. Maybe a little bit of love and lots of happy and—

A future.

Building their lives together, one piece at a time.

———

WILL

He'd helped clean up Brit's place after eating an obscene amount of pie.

But now he didn't have any other reason to delay heading home.

Lily had gone hours before.

And he'd forced himself to stay, to pretend to be happy and enjoying himself.

But all he'd been thinking about was the tiny blond pixie who drove him to insanity.

Absolute fucking insanity.

She had for years.

She had since childhood.

But he hadn't seen her since she was twelve and he was going off to make it big.

He'd gotten there eventually, and she...

Hell, she'd turned into a *woman.*

Tiny, still with that shock of blond hair. But, holy hell, did she have curves that tempted and called to the male side of him.

He wanted to strip her naked, to see and caress, to touch and lick and stroke every inch of her. He was desperate for it, actually.

But she was off-limits.

Not even because she worked for the team—though that was an argument in of itself. Though, it was an argument that was kind of pointless considering how much back office staff and the players mixed.

The bigger reason she was off-limits was because she was the daughter of the man who'd been more of a father figure to him than his sperm donor ever had.

Sighing, he shoved a hand through his hair.

She'd liked him when she'd been twelve and he was sixteen.

Too many years between them, and it hadn't even been on his radar then. Her childhood crush something that amused.

But when Tim had called him, told him that Lily had been hired by the Gold, he'd been ecstatic. It had been too long since he'd seen her, too long since he'd been home to visit the family that had become his in the year he'd lived with them.

Then he'd actually picked Lily up at the airport.

And everything had gone wrong.

Wrong.

Because she'd walked out from the terminal and he'd recognized her immediately and—

Holy fucking shit, every single cell in his body had stood up and taken notice.

And the ones in his dick—

Well, *those* had encouraged him to claim.

Fucking stupid.

Fucking *dangerous.*

Dangerous enough that he'd pushed all of that desire out of his brain and shoved her firmly back into the metal box that was coded as sister.

Sister.

Completely and totally off-limits.

Not sexual.

Not touchable.

Not lickable or strokeable or fuckable.

His dick twitched.

"Fuck," he muttered, sending threats to the offending organ, advising it to behave, otherwise he'd punish it.

Something it didn't give a fuck about.

Because punishment meant jerking himself off until he was so drained that his dick couldn't get hard, even at the thought of sexy, pixie Lily.

His dick liked *that* punishment very much.

And hell, so did the rest of him.

But besides the attraction he would never be able to act on, the bigger issue might be that he was talking to his dick, treating it like it was a whole different person.

Sighing, he pulled into his driveway, into his garage, closing the large metal door behind him. His mom had decided at the last minute that she didn't want to fly over Christmas, so he would grab a flight back home to Minnesota in a few days to catch up with her before the team's Christmas break was completed.

But tomorrow, he'd spend Christmas Eve alone.

And then after that, Christmas Day alone.

And...well, aside from the time he had with his teammates, Will was used to spending lots of time alone.

It wasn't a big deal.

Or at least, that was what he told himself when the loneliness crept in, choking him, making his skin feel too tight for his body, making it hard for him to breathe.

He was used to that, too.

Single mom.

Kid at home alone a lot.

Hockey was an outlet, but he couldn't horn in on his teammates every single day. They had lives and kids and pets and women.

So, he shoved it down, breathed through the vice tightening around his lungs, and he lived his life.

Tonight, though, he just wanted to go to bed. He wanted to sleep and forget about the loneliness and the fact that he would be spending Christmas alone with his Xbox and his palm, creating callouses from all the button pushing and jerking off. Maybe those behaviors weren't very much aligned with the holiday spirit, but that was what he had.

All that he had.

So as soon as the garage was closed up, he turned off the engine, got out, and slammed the car door.

He walked into his house.

Scrabbled along the wall until he found the switch—something he struggled with, even though he'd been living there for months.

Finally, he felt the right switch, pressed it, and the kitchen lights flicked on.

And Will nearly jumped right the fuck out of his skin when he saw that Lily was sitting at his kitchen island.

———

Thank you for reading! I hope you loved Jordyn and Ben as much as I did! The next book in the Gold Hockey series is CRUSHED. **She was everything he shouldn't want. He was going to take her anyway.**

CLICK HERE TO GET CRUSHED NOW>

And if you enjoyed COVERED, you'll love the bad boys of the Rush! This brand new hockey trilogy begins with BIG PUCK ENERGY. *I played hard, and lived even harder...*

CLICK HERE TO READ BIG PUCK ENERGY NOW>

———

Big Puck Energy

AXEL

I groaned and tried valiantly to open my eyes, but my head was pounding, so the moment light passed my lids, I slammed them closed again.

"Fuck," I muttered, running a hand over my face—

Or trying to.

Because it was impossible.

No, not *impossible*. I frowned, forced my lids open, ignoring the sunlight stabbing at my brain.

Only *one* was impossible because...it was handcuffed to some sort of rail above my head. The other hand was at my side, pinned half under my ass. *That* one was just numb, and I moved it carefully, nerves prickling, tingles shooting up my arm.

What kind of freaky shit had I gotten into last night?

I squinted, trying to remember, but not able to recall anything more than swatches of noise and things breaking and booze going down smoother and smoother.

Until it had tasted like water.

That's probably why it hurt so much to open my eyes today.

A foot kicked mine, and not lightly either.

"Ow," I muttered, glancing up and squinting at the sun. Someone was standing there, not that I could see more than a wavering black silhouette.

"Whatcha doing down there?"

Female.

My mind perked up. My brain focused enough for the wavering shadow to steady, to turn into something...delicious.

Small. Curvy. *Delicious*.

"Depends." I said, curving my lips into the smile that had gotten me pussy from the time I was fifteen. "You coming down here to experience it?"

Silence.

Long and quiet enough that I could hear the birds chirping and the insects buzzing, and seriously, what the fuck time of the day was it?

I hadn't been up this early in...

I couldn't remember. Or maybe I *could* have remembered if the woman standing over me hadn't started laughing. Not a gentle, quiet, tinkling laugh like so many of the puck bunnies that hung at the rink and wanted a piece of me before I hit it big, but a loud and hearty guffaw that shouldn't have been sexy and yet somehow was.

Roughened velvet.

I wanted to fuck her, and I hadn't even seen her face.

But hell, the way the shadows had coalesced into something curvy and petite paired with that sexy unhindered laugh, and I was hard.

"Baby—" I began.

The *click* of a shotgun cocking had my mind rocketing well away from my dick.

Okay, this wasn't nearly as amusing.

Or sexy.

"Hold on a—" I tried.

The laugh had disappeared, taut intensity had surrounded him. "I'm going to talk." Deadly words. "And you're going to speak when I give you permission to do so."

Ice. Orders.

They both began prickling down my nape, curling in my stomach like a poisonous snake prepared to strike.

Meh.

Just call me Steve Irwin.

Of course...there was also that sting ray.

And I had a shotgun pointed at my head.

So...right. I kept my snark locked (albeit loaded, *heh*). The sun, on the other hand, was a total bitch, and since I was tired of squinting against it, I dropped my gaze to my feet.

The woman nudged me with her foot again—this time hard enough to hurt. "I'd advise that you keep your eyes on mine."

"I would," I said, getting frustrated now, that snake darting forward and baring its fangs as I stupidly reached out to grab it, "if I could fucking see you instead of burning my fucking irises by staring into the *sun!*"

Silence.

Shit.

I clenched my teeth against an apology and waited, trying to hold back a wince, expecting the shotgun to go off.

Instead, she surprised me by stepping to the side so that I could look up at her and see something besides blinding white light.

Blinking a few times to steady my vision, I felt my cock get even harder.

Fuck.

She was a porn film come to life.

A cowboy hat on her head, a low-cut white tank covered by a flannel only halfway buttoned up, skintight jeans, and boots.

Not cowboy boots, but sturdy, brown leather boots with bright red laces.

They were well-worn. They were dirty.

They did *not* fit with the curvy little woman in front of me.

"Baby—"

The gun leveled at my chest.

"I don't believe I gave you permission to speak," she gritted out.

Probably, I should shut up, but I'd never been great with authority or people telling me what to do. "I don't believe I asked *you* to wake me up and point a shotgun at me," I snapped.

Slowly, she lifted one hand and tilted back her hat.

That snake coiled again.

Only this time, I could admit it was coiled in the corner in fear, hoping to not be provoked, because it wasn't sure it would survive if it struck again.

"Well," she said lightly, "I normally point shotguns at people who show up unwelcome on my porch, but I *especially* point shotguns at those who show up unwelcome *and* spend their free time tearing up my town." The gun didn't waver, not in the least. "So, what the fuck are you doing here, Axel Finnigan?"

Come to think of it, I didn't *know* what I was doing here.

Last I remembered, I'd been cuddled up to a rather tall blonde and her hands had been sliding beneath the waistband of my jeans.

Had I fucked her?

I couldn't remember.

And it hurt too much when I tried to, so I just let it go. The blonde wouldn't be the first girl I didn't remember sleeping with. If I was being truthful—something I despised—she also probably wouldn't be the last.

"I don't know," I said, squinting against the sun and trying to actually see where I was. I should also probably be sorting out how I'd become handcuffed to the railing, but...meh.

I'd been in stranger scenarios.

One time I'd woken up floating in a pool, naked, sunburned to hell and precariously perched on one of those inflatable rafts shaped like a giant pineapple. Another time, I'd woken up naked and with half a watermelon (half-eaten to go with the theme) over my junk. Still once more, I'd peeled back my lids and woken up between three nude people—*people* because only two of them female.

The common theme was nakedness.

Yeah, yeah I liked to take off my clothes.

But I had a nice body, and *people* didn't seem to mind.

Not to mention, I grew up in locker rooms, grew up with stall showers where shyness and covering my junk wasn't necessary. I'd seen more dick than most porn stars, but it was part of the game —well, not the game so much as the cleaning up process afterward.

As was the partying and the waking up naked—and sometimes still drunk.

Not much fazed me. Not the dicks or the nakedness or the women and booze. Every time I'd ever woken up in a pesky scenario, I'd just shrugged, dragged my sorry ass out of there and stumbled home.

Sometimes remembering (the watermelon had been a joke by my linemate). Sometimes not (like not remembering if I fucked the blonde from last night).

But I'd never woken up like this.

First, I wasn't clothed.

Second, I was handcuffed.

Third, I was staring down the barrel of gun, the other side held by a gorgeous woman who appeared to be looking for any excuse to pull the trigger.

"You don't know," she said slowly, as though I were an idiot.

And maybe I was. I hadn't gone to college. I'd barely graduated high school. I was good at exactly three things—hockey, fucking, and drinking.

The middle skill was what prompted my next reply.

"Do you have a bondage fantasy?" I asked, rattling the cuff. "Because I'd be happy to oblige."

The gun dropped further...pointing at my dick.

I watched her finger tighten on the trigger, and I felt fear—*real fear*—for the first time in a long, *long* time.

But I couldn't even push out the request to ask her not to shoot me.

All I *could* do was stand there and watch and cringe and . . . *wait.*

Just when I thought she was definitely going to fire, she spun on her heel, stomped back across the porch, and disappeared into the house.

The door slammed.

And silence descended again.

CLICK HERE TO READ BIG PUCK ENERGY NOW>

———

And don't forget to dive into the the sexy, sweet, and close-knit Breakers Hockey crew. <u>The first book in the series, BROKEN, is now live!</u>
It is sexy, hot, adorable and such a fun read. You will not be able to put this down!" —Amazon Reviewer

———

I so appreciate your help in spreading the word about my books, including sharing with friends! Please leave a review on your favorite book site!

You can also join my Facebook group, the Fabinators, for exclusive giveaways and sneak peeks of future books.

SIGN UP FOR ELISE FABER'S NEWSLETTER HERE:
https://www.elisefaber.com/newsletter

———

Hate missing Elise's new releases? Love contests, exclusive excerpts and giveaways?

Then signup for Elise's newsletter here!

www.elisefaber.com/newsletter

———

And join Elise's fan group, the Fabinators (https://www. facebook.com/groups/fabinators) for insider information, sneak peaks at new releases, and fun freebies! Hope to see you there!

———

GOLD HOCKEY SERIES

Gold Hockey (all stand alone)
Blocked
Backhand
Boarding
Benched
Breakaway
Breakout
Checked
Coasting
Centered
Charging
Caged
Crashed
A Gold Christmas
Cycled
Caught
Cap
Covered
Crushed

ALSO BY ELISE FABER

***Billionaire's Club* (all stand alone)**

Bad Night Stand

Bad Breakup

Bad Husband

Bad Hookup

Bad Divorce

Bad Fiancé

Bad Boyfriend

Bad Blind Date

Bad Wedding

Bad Engagement

Bad Bridesmaid

Bad Swipe

Bad Girlfriend

Bad Best Friend

Bad Billionaire's Quickies

***Gold Hockey* (all stand alone)**

Blocked

Backhand

Boarding

Benched

Breakaway

Breakout

Checked

Coasting

Centered

Charging

Caged

Crashed

A Gold Christmas

Cycled

Caught

Cap

Covered

Breakers Hockey (all stand alone)

<u>Broken</u>

<u>Boldly</u>

<u>Breathless</u>

<u>Ballsy</u>

Rush Hockey

Big Puck Energy

Filthy Puckboy

So Pucking Over It

Love, Action, Camera (all stand alone)

Dotted Line

Action Shot

Close-Up

End Scene

Meet Cute

***Love After Midnight* (all stand alone)**

Rum And Notes

Virgin Daiquiri

On The Rocks

Sex On The Seats

Life Sucks Series (all stand alone)

Train Wreck

Hot Mess

Dumpster Fire

Clusterf*@k

FUBAR

Roosevelt Ranch Series (all stand alone, series complete)

Disaster at Roosevelt Ranch

Heartbreak at Roosevelt Ranch

Collision at Roosevelt Ranch

Regret at Roosevelt Ranch

Desire at Roosevelt Ranch

Phoenix Series (read in order)

Phoenix Rising

Dark Phoenix

Phoenix Freed

Phoenix: LexTal Chronicles (rereleasing soon, stand alone, Phoenix world)

From Ashes

In Flames

To Smoke

KTS Series (all stand alone, series complete)

Riding The Edge

Crossing The Line

Leveling The Field

Scorching The Earth

Cocky Heroes World

Tattooed Troublemaker

About the Author

USA Today bestselling author, Elise Faber, loves chocolate, Star Wars, Harry Potter, and hockey (the order depending on the day and how well her team -- the Sharks! -- are playing). She and her husband also play as much hockey as they can squeeze into their schedules, so much so that their typical date night is spent on the ice. Elise is the mom to two exuberant boys and lives in Northern California. Connect with her in her Facebook group, the Fabinators or find more information about her books at www.elise-faber.com.

facebook.com/elisefaberauthor

amazon.com/author/elisefaber

bookbub.com/profile/elise-faber

instagram.com/elisefaber

tiktok.com/@elisefaberauthor

goodreads.com/elisefaber

www.ingramcontent.com/pod-product-compliance
Lightning Source LLC
Chambersburg PA
CBHW071553110726

47908CB00007B/2088